When disaster turns to passion

Welcome to an exciting new series of twelve books
from Silhouette®, 36 HOURS, where danger is just a
heartbeat away. Unprecedented rainstorms cause a
36 hour blackout in Grand Springs and it sets off a
string of events that alters people's lives forever...

This month look for:

Marriage by Contract by Sandra Steffen—
A tiny baby waits for a home, while a single woman
yearns for a child. So a daring doctor makes a
dramatic proposal.

Partners in Crime by Alicia Scott—
A world-weary detective has a sexy suspect in a
murder investigation, but does the passion he finds in
her arms convince him that she's innocent?

Alicia Scott

recently escaped the corporate world to pursue her writing full-time. According to the former consultant, 'I've been a writer for as long as I can remember. For me, it's the perfect job, and you can't beat the dress code.' Born in Hawaii, she grew up in Oregon before moving to Massachusetts. Recent winner of the *Romantic Times* award for Career Achievement in Series Romantic Suspense, she spends her time chasing after two feisty felines, eating chocolate and running around the globe. Alicia also writes mainstream romantic suspense as Lisa Gardner.

Alicia loves to hear from readers! You can reach her at P.O. Box 1667, Framingham, MA 10701-1667, USA.

36 Hours

When disaster turns to passion

PARTNERS
IN CRIME

Alicia Scott

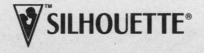
™ SILHOUETTE®

*Silhouette and Colophon are registered trademarks of
Harlequin Books S.A., used under licence.*

*First published in Great Britain 1999
Silhouette Books, Eton House, 18-24 Paradise Road,
Richmond, Surrey TW9 1SR*

© Harlequin Books S.A. 1997

Special thanks and acknowledgement are given to Alicia Scott
for her contribution to the 36 HOURS series.

ISBN 0 373 65014 0

105-9907

*Printed and bound in Spain
by Litografia Rosés S.A., Barcelona*

36 Hours

When disaster turns to passion

For the residents of Grand Springs, the
storm-induced blackout was just the beginning…

Each book stands alone, but together they're terrific!

Special thanks to Jenn Carson R.N., first for helping me find the perfect poison, and second for being the best college room-mate and lifelong friend a person could have. Also, to my grandparents, who endured the Tillamook flood and mudslides of 1995 with enough examples of courage, compassion and community to fill many, many, many books. You inspire me.

Prologue

After midnight, most people in Grand Springs were safely tucked in bed. The hospital still hummed with life, of course. Lately, the police department, as well. But most people in the quiet community were in bed by eleven, and most of the ranchers were in bed well before that.

That's why Josie liked midnight so well. No more phones jangling with questions from the local business-people who'd watched their dreams swept away in just thirty-six hours of rain, mud slides and lightning. No more farmers, standing before her desk in their mud-splattered boots and well-broken-in jeans, slowly twisting the brims of their hats as they asked her how they were supposed to get their cows through the winter when their fields were so buried in silt and mud it would take twelve months of expensive rehabilitation before they'd be fit to grow hay again. No more Hal Stuart demanding yet another cut of Grand Springs's budget because he was acting mayor, dammit, and when he said jump, you'd better say "How high?"

Late at night, Josie could shut the door of her treasurer's office, take the phone off the hook and finally get work done. She figured and refigured the cost of the flooding and power outage. She looked at pictures of the holes that had appeared in the mountain passes, whole chunks of road swept away by mud slides. She pondered the impact on families, not all of whom were insured, and especially on the farmers who'd never thought to buy flood insurance—then watched half of their cows drown in water that just wouldn't stop.

Josie didn't have easy answers. She couldn't get the county commissioners to focus on the complex ones. So she worked until three or four in the morning most nights, trying to bring order to the chaos. And she pretended that when she finally went home to sleep, she didn't still see Olivia, her best friend and Grand Springs's indomitable mayor, dying in her arms while the world raged and howled around them.

Her eyes grew blurry as 2:00 a.m. came and went. She pored over information on federal aid programs. She read about the adopt-a-farm programs other states had used to weather such disasters. She jotted down notes on the strip mining information Hal wanted. She wrote herself a reminder on the upcoming Band, Bingo, Bake Sale fundraiser next week.

She tried valiantly to keep her eyes open.

The pen slipped from between her fingers. Her head nodded against her chest. Her red, exhausted eyes gave in and closed.

She slid down into her chair, and the sleep hit her all at once and with a fury.

Dark clouds teeming rain. The sky booming and cracking with a vengeful electrical storm. The thunder so close it echoed through the exposed-beam hallway of the Squaw Creek Lodge.

Josie ran down the hall. Searching, searching, searching. Hal's wedding was about to begin. Where was Olivia? Olivia would never be late for her own son's wedding.

She had to find Olivia. The foreboding rolled in her stomach like an echo of the storm, dark and horrible.

A blurry shape in white brushed her shoulder. The bride. Randi, Hal Stuart's bride, running down the hall. Why was the bride running away from the wedding?

Thunder cracked. The lodge shuddered. Another boom and the lodge plunged into blackness.

A cry. "The bride has disappeared!"

Chaos.

The glow of a candle abruptly appeared, illuminating the end of the hallway. Josie ran toward it. She saw Hal, pale and harried. She heard more voices. "My God, I think she's unconscious!" In the distance, someone's beeper went off.

Where was Olivia?

Suddenly the lodge was gone. She was out in the night, the wind buffeting her practical economy car, the rain slapping her windshield. Her long blond hair had been ripped free from its knot and was now plastered against her cheeks. Her favorite black cocktail suit, drenched and ruined, clung to her skin.

She drove, the road lights out, the streets flooded, the storm fierce and merciless.

Olivia, Olivia, Olivia. She had to find Olivia.

She reached Olivia's street. She turned into the darkened drive. The wind howled.

No lights appeared on in the house. Not even the reassuring flicker of a candle. Black, black house. Dark, dark night.

For a moment, Josie was frozen by her own fear.

I know what's in that house. I know what I'm going to find.

Her dream lurched, twisted, then turned on itself like a cannibal.

The storm was gone. The sky was clear, blue, gentle with spring. She was twelve years old, pushing open the gate of the white picket fence, walking up the drive of their suburban home. Cutoff jeans left her long legs bare and nut brown. Her simple white T-shirt billowed comfortably around her arms. She was barefoot. She was humming.

"Mom, I'm home!"

Her dream lurched again, and the whipping wind made her stagger back.

Josie fought her way to Olivia's back door. She peered through the window as the lightning cracked.

Twist.

Flipping her blond ponytail out of her way, she skipped through the back door, eager to tell her mother about her day—

Twist.

Olivia, sprawled on the elegant black-and-white kitchen floor, prostrate in a sea of teal-colored silk.

Josie fumbled with the knob. She cried out her friend's name. She raised her fist and prepared to smash the window.

The door opened in her hand, unlocked all along, and she rushed into the house.

Twist.

The scent of fresh-baked cookies and spring tulips. The warm, familiar undertones of vanilla and nutmeg. She walked through the kitchen, wondering why her mother wasn't sitting at the simple block wood table the way she usually did, then passed through the kitchen into the entryway. Stopping. Freezing. Crying.

"Mom? Mom? *Mommy!*"

Twist.

"Olivia! Dear God, Olivia!"

Her friend was motionless on the floor and the scent of gardenias was cloying and thick.

Josie fell to her knees, shaking her best friend's shoulders. Olivia didn't move.

Dear God, Josie couldn't find a pulse.

"Don't die on me," she whispered. *"Please, please, don't die on me. You're the only person I've trusted. The only person who's believed in me. Olivia…"*

Twist.

The feel of the old hardwood floors against her tender knees. The scent of the lemon beeswax her mother used to polish what life she could into the old floors. Little Josie touched her mother's beautiful gold hair and felt the chill on her cooling skin.

Keening, sobbing, crying. Rocking back and forth, not knowing what to do. Her mom looked so beautiful, her golden hair pooled around her, her white cotton dress draped around her twisted limbs. Her blue eyes, so much like Josie's, were open. But they stared sightlessly at the ceiling, and would never blink again.

"I'm sorry, Mom. I'm sorry, I'm sorry."

Twist.

"*Think, Josie, think—911. Call 911!*"

She grabbed the cordless phone from the kitchen counter. No dial tone. The power outage had rendered it useless. She threw it across the room. Another bolt of lightning seared the kitchen. She spotted Olivia's purse on the kitchen table. The cellular phone.

Josie grabbed the purse. She pawed through it then turned it over and dumped out the flip phone. Dial, dial, dial.

"*Please, I need an ambulance. I think she's dead.*"

The dispatcher asked questions. Josie fumbled through answers. She checked for noticeable injuries. She began to administer CPR. She hunched over her best friend's body, massaged her chest and tried to will the life back into her.

Live, live, live.

Sirens cut through the roaring night. Then the jangle of EMTs sounded down the sidewalk. Dimly, she heard herself cry, "In here, in here. Breathe, Olivia! Damn you, breathe!"

The EMTs rushed into the kitchen. They pushed her aside, then hunched over Olivia, muttering to each other, continuing with CPR.

"Let's move."

Suddenly they had Olivia strapped to the stretcher. They were rolling away, back into the horrible night. Josie wanted to go in the ambulance. She wanted to hold Olivia's hand and beg her to live.

The EMTs left Josie behind. She stood in the rain, watching the ambulance disappear, reaching out her hands. The storm continued. She didn't notice it anymore.

Live. Live. Live.

Twist.

I'm sorry. I'm sorry. I'm sorry.

Josie jerked awake at her desk. She rubbed her temples furiously, then scrubbed at the moisture now staining her cheeks. It didn't help. The images remained behind her eyelids, the past and present too intertwined to be separated.

And all the work in the world, all the nightmares in the world, didn't change the outcome of either night.

Olivia had died at the hospital. A heart attack was the initial ruling. But days later, Detective Stone Richardson raised some questions, and further investigation revealed that she'd been poisoned—someone had thrust a hypodermic full of undiluted potassium into her leg, causing nearly instant cardiac arrest.

Olivia had been murdered, and nothing in Grand Springs had been the same.

Death. Pain. Betrayal.

I didn't do it, I didn't do it, Josie reminded herself. Sitting alone in her shadowed office, however, she still couldn't escape her next thought.

Not this time.

One

"Uh-oh. Here comes trouble."

"Hmm?" Detective Jack Stryker lifted his scrunched eyes from the coroner's report and belatedly followed his partner's gaze. "Damn."

"Just what we need," Detective Stone Richardson agreed, "like a hound dog needs a flea."

"At least fleas don't campaign for your vote—they know they're a nuisance." Jack sighed. He tucked the coroner's report back into the Olivia Stuart file with a last glance of frustration and longing. The answers were in there somewhere, he just knew it. He'd missed something the first time around, made a mistake. He didn't screw up often, but he must have this time, because it had been more than three months and they still had no leads on the Olivia Stuart case.

And now Hal Stuart, acting mayor of Grand Springs and one of the most annoying men God had ever created, had entered the police station. He wove through the corridor like a tin soldier, his arms held tightly against his double-breasted suit as if he didn't want to touch anything—the dirt might rub off.

Hal Stuart didn't come to the police station often—Jack figured it was too long on chaos and too short on decoration for his taste. The plain corridor poured into the main room, comprised of a beat-up wood floor, numerous metal desks and one wall of windows. In the corner, the lone office belonged to Frank Sanderson, the chief of police. It was as bare bones and worn as the rest of the place. As Sanderson had informed Hal during his last visit, he had better things to do than pick out wallpaper.

Grand Springs was becoming a big city in many ways, and it had a growing drug problem and overworked police department to prove it. Now it also had the murder of Grand Springs's mayor, Olivia Stuart, making the pressure even more intense.

Jack planted his feet on the floor and summoned a last deep breath. He was tired—he often worked until ten at night, then brought work home with him—but it didn't show. He'd already smoothed his face into the bland, capable expression cops wore for outsiders. He'd learned a lot about how to handle politicians over the years.

Stone, who prided himself on irreverence, leaned back and propped up his feet on his desk in a deliberately casual pose.

"Don't antagonize him," Jack ordered under his breath as Hal entered the main room. "It just encourages him to talk more."

"But baiting him is the only sport I get around here."

"It's not a sport—to be a sport, it would have to be a challenge."

Stone was still chuckling softly when Hal planted himself in front of their desks. The acting mayor's soft features were already screwed into a scowl. His blond hair, normally carefully smoothed back, looked mussed, and his tailored suit was uncharacteristically disarrayed. Someone, Jack thought, must be making the acting mayor actually work. Judging by the look on his face, he wasn't happy about it, either.

"Howdy, Hal," Stone sang out. "Nice of you to drop on by. Did you bring us poor slaving public servants any lunch?"

Hal's frown grew, the look in his eyes uncertain. He crossed his arms over his chest and adopted a firm expression.

"No. Look, I'm a very busy man, so let's make this quick—"

"Of course," Stone said politely. Jack hid his wince behind a small cough. When Hal said "let's make this quick" it meant it was going to be long.

"I've given you three months!" Hal announced. "In the beginning, everything was upside down from the power outage, I understood that. Then there were the immediate needs of restoring order and policing the streets after the ensuing accidents and incidents. But it's late September now. The other situations are in the past, and I want to know—why isn't my mother's case being given top priority?"

"It is," Jack said. He didn't need a lecture on his job. He already knew that the chances of solving a three-and-a-half-month-old murder case were slim. It ate away at him every night as he pored over old case notes, wondering why they couldn't connect the dots.

"Then, you have new leads to report?"

"No," Stone said. "But we've processed forty-six people for vandalism and theft, fifteen men for drunken and disorderly conduct, and six people for brawling. Plus, we've worked on finding your vanished bride as well as the mother who abandoned her baby at the hospital, and then your sister, Eve, and her daughter, Molly, when they were kidnapped. We've also worked on discovering the true identity of Martin Smith, evacuating people from unstable areas and delivering supplies to people cut off by the mud slides. Oh, and I foiled a bank robbery. A pretty slow summer here in Grand Springs, wouldn't you say, Stryker?"

"We're giving the investigation everything we can,"

Jack translated for Hal. He gave Stone a meaningful look that his partner ignored.

"Didn't Randi give you a name? What more do you require?" Randi Howell was Hal's former fiancée. She'd fled on their wedding day due to her own misgivings…and two thugs who had caught her eavesdropping on their conversation.

"Randi reported that she overhead one of the men say, 'Jo will take care of the broad—it's her specialty.' The statement's too vague," Jack said matter-of-factly. "We can't be sure they were talking about Olivia. We can't even be sure 'take care of the broad' means murder. And we have no idea who 'Jo' is."

"As far as we know, Jo could be an acupuncture specialist," Stone volunteered. "We can't arrest everyone named Jo based on a statement like that."

Hal's face reddened. He turned on Stone. "And your friend the psychic woman, doesn't she know anything else? Or is she talking to Elvis instead these days?"

Jack placed his hand on Stone's arm to keep him sitting. As Hal well knew, Jessica Hanson was a little more than Stone's friend. She was now his wife. And she wasn't exactly a psychic. The visions she'd experienced after hitting her head during the blackout in June had stopped, and no one was certain why they had happened or what they had meant.

For a bit, however, Jessica had been plagued by the image of a tall, blond woman stabbing a hypodermic needle into Olivia's leg. These "visions" were always followed by the scent of gardenias.

Hal had been informed of all this. He had also been told that someone had sent a bowl of gardenias as a funeral bouquet to Olivia Stuart's house. The flowers hadn't included a card and Eve Stuart, Hal's sister, could only vaguely recall an elegantly dressed blonde standing in the doorway with the bowl. Stone had tested the bowl for fingerprints. Nothing.

Jack said now, "As you know, Hal, we followed up on Jessica's 'visions.' Stone had the doctors examine the body, and the autopsy confirmed that Olivia had been injected with a dose of pure potassium, leading to immediate cardiac arrest. That's all Jessica saw and it's been noted."

"You can't trace the poison?"

"No."

"Why not? I thought you had computers for that sort of thing. Labs? What the hell is our budget paying for these days, anyway?"

Jack grew tired. They'd had this conversation before. Nothing had changed. For a moment, Jack contemplated telling the man they'd get a lot further a lot faster if he'd shut up and leave them alone. Of course, he said no such thing. "Straight Arrow Stryker" never lost control.

"Pure potassium is readily accessible," he intoned quietly. "All hospitals commonly administer it in a diluted form to patients recovering from surgery. According to the doctors, it's available at all nursing stations in a hospital, and the nursing stations are unlocked and unmonitored.

"We interviewed all the hospital staff, and no one remembers noticing any potassium missing. Of course, the potassium may have come from an outside hospital. It might have been ordered directly from a medical supply store. At this point, there's no way to know."

"You can't tell a brand or a batch or something like that?"

"If we had a bottle or label, maybe we could. If we had a needle, we could trace the parts, the manufacturer, maybe get prints or DNA. But we don't. We just have a victim with a potassium level over ten mils per liter. We have a crime scene with no signs of a forced entry. There are no latent or patent prints. We have no hair, no fiber. At this point, the most likely suspect is Casper the Friendly

Ghost.'' Jack's voice ended with an edge. He and Stone
had the highest arrest record in Grand Springs, dammit.
They were good, they were serious, they were committed.
*So how could they not determine who murdered such a
fine woman as Olivia Stuart?*

''But...but...'' Hal was struggling now. Jack couldn't
tell if it was from honest emotion or just frustration. Hal
wasn't a particularly strong man, but he was hard to read.
He said abruptly, ''What about my mother's last word?''

''Coal?'' Stone shrugged. ''To tell you the truth, we're
just not sure. My personal theory is that she was talking
about the strip mining debates. She was really against strip
mining in Grand Springs, just like you're really for it....''

Hal stiffened. Now his face was definitely shuttered.
He'd been taking some heat on the subject, particularly
from Rio Redtree, top investigative reporter for the *Grand
Springs Herald.* ''I sold my stock in the companies. And
I've asked Josie to look into both the advantages and *dis-
advantages* of permitting strip mining in Grand Springs.
I'm a fair man.'' He paused, his eyes narrowing. ''Do...do
you think one of those companies might have something
to do with my mother's death?''

Jack glanced at Stone. They'd argued this matter numerous times without reaching a conclusion. Jack didn't
believe a person would refer to a political debate as her
last word. He also wasn't a big fan of conspiracy theories.
Stone felt the strip mining companies had enough to gain
from Olivia's death to make them likely suspects.

''It's possible,'' Jack said carefully, ''but not probable.
The cause of death was poison, and statistically speaking,
poison is a 'personal' MO—we see wives murdering husbands, a jealous lover spiking a rival's drink, that sort of
thing. For poison to be used in a hit... That would be
unusual.''

''Then go out and interview everyone she knew!''

''We did. We asked you for a list of associates, remember, Hal?'' Jack said. ''Then we talked to everyone on that list. Business associates, neighbors, friends, family. I have the interview notes right here.''

''And?''

''And we don't have any substantial suspects. Olivia was a well-respected mayor, friend and mother. Even her political opponents thought highly of her. She was a good woman, Hal. Her loss is deeply felt.''

Hal looked away. Maybe the emotion was genuine, after all. ''You know, there were no 'intimates' on that list, Hal,'' Jack said quietly. ''No past boyfriends, romantic interests. Can you think of anyone, maybe a jilted lover—''

''Olivia? Date?'' Hal laughed harshly. ''My mother was much too sophisticated for the men in this town. And she was tougher than all of them.''

Abruptly, Hal planted his hands on Jack's desk. ''Let me spell it out for you. I did my part. I've given you all the information you've asked for, and I've given you more than three months to get results. Well it's almost the end of September, detectives, and you have *nothing*. I'm not impressed. The taxpayers of this town are not impressed. And the budget for the police department is about to come up for review....''

Stone's feet dropped to the floor. He was half out of his chair before Jack pulled him back down.

''Understood. And I tell you again, Hal, there's no one who wants to solve this case more than we do. No one.''

''Huh.'' Hal's expression was blatantly unconvinced. Jack had to dig his fingers into Stone's arm while Hal glanced at his watch. ''Thirty minutes are up. I have to get to my next meeting with Jo—''

''Mayor? Call on line one,'' the receptionist interrupted.

Hal grunted and took the call. He shook his head, said he'd get to it in a minute, sighed and hung up. ''Incompetence,'' he muttered. ''Sheer incompetence.''

Jack studied Hal for a long time. Stone had gone still beside him. "Your meeting with Jo?" he asked quietly. Was the man so dense he could not see the significance of his own words?

"Jo? Oh, Josie Reynolds. You know Josie." Hal headed toward the door. Jack and Stone didn't stop him.

Stone waited until the acting mayor was completely out of sight before speaking. "Josie Reynolds. Do you think…?"

"We interviewed her, right?" Jack was pawing through the notes. "She discovered the body. She called 911. The EMTs said she'd started CPR before they arrived."

"I was the one who talked to her, I remember now. Ah, hell, I don't know, Stryker. She was pretty broken up, you could tell she and Olivia had been close. I heard Olivia had been the one to give Josie the job as treasurer. She took Josie under her wing, made her feel at home." Stone contemplated his thoughts. "You've met her, right? I've seen her around, at the usual places, but I'd never really spoken to her before Olivia's death." He grinned abruptly. "Odd, you know, for a man like me not to approach a beautiful lady. But…well, she seems to keep to herself. As much as it wounds me to admit it, I'm not sure she would have considered me her type."

Jack nodded. He had been introduced to Josie Reynolds two years ago when she'd taken the job as town treasurer, and she wasn't the kind of woman a man forgot. Five foot six with a cloud of blond hair and frank blue eyes, she looked more like a beauty queen than a CPA. By all accounts, however, she was good. Olivia had described her as spirited, passionate, and committed. She got her job done. That was about all Stryker knew. He had always made it a point to stay clear of Josie Reynolds, though he could never say why. And not once in the past two years, in all the times their paths had crossed, had she ever approached him. Without saying a word, they seemed to have settled upon a policy of mutually-agreed avoidances. He kept to his side of the room. She kept to hers.

Stone rose to his feet. "Hungry? I think they can hear my stomach in Wichita by now."

Jack automatically shook his head.

Stone knew better. "Hey, Straight Arrow, when was the last time you ate?"

"I'm fine."

"If you're fine then I'm ugly—and we both know I'm not ugly. I've seen that look in your eye, Jack. You're in bulldog mode and have been for weeks. How many of those files are you bringin' home at night? How many times are you gonna pore over them with your face scrunched up? You get any more lines in your forehead and people will mistake you for a road map."

"You're not exactly lolling around popping bonbons."

"Nope. But I got smart. I married Jessie." Stone beamed, Jack rolled his eyes. Stone was so gaga over his new wife, it made a man ill. Jack honestly wished Stone the best and he liked Jessie, but having been married once before himself, he never intended on having Sucker stamped on his forehead again.

"Go meet Jessica for lunch," Jack said sagely.

"Is that an order, boss man? You know I'd do anything for my partner."

Jack just grunted.

"I'm telling you, Jack, you're too intense." Stone gathered up his sport coat. "Unwind a little, smell the roses. Take a beautiful woman out to dinner. It'll put a skip in your step."

"That's what Grand Springs needs right now—skipping detectives."

"Absolutely. I'll be back in an hour. Feel free to solve the case while I'm gone."

"I'll do that."

Stone waved, but Jack didn't wave back. He had his

nose buried in the files, looking for Josie Reynolds's interview notes. Josie Reynolds. Jo. Josie.

Josie Reynolds whom he had always avoided. And yet he always knew exactly where she was in a crowded room. Stryker set down his pencil. No more reading. He would talk to her in person. And he would closely watch her eyes.

Josie Reynolds had never met Gabe Chouder, but she knew him. In the last three months it seemed she had met all the Gabe Chouders of the world, and now as he stood before her desk, she wondered if she would be able to help him any more than she'd helped the others.

Gabe owned a small dairy farm outside of Grand Springs. Two hundred and fifty-four dairy cows on a spread that had belonged to his family for three generations. Now most of those fields were under three feet of mud and silt. His grain silo was destroyed. The water-soaked straw and alfalfa bales had been hauled away before they spontaneously combusted and burned down the little Gabe had left.

When the flood warnings had been issued, Gabe and his son had rounded up the cows, while his two daughters had tended the calves. The cows had been lined up in the milking parlor, which was set on higher ground. He'd done this before, he told Josie, and it had always worked. Grand Springs's valley didn't flood much or deeply. The rivers in his low-lying land overran some springs when the snow thawed too fast. Maybe he'd get a foot or two of water.

But the storm had hit; the skies opened up and poured into swollen rivers. Banks had given way. Mountainsides already at saturation point hadn't been able to take any more. In a span of thirty-six hours, Mother Nature had burst and Gabe Chouder's life would never be the same.

The water had risen three feet in a matter of hours. He and his son had raised the calves into the hayloft, but below, their cows had bawled in terror as lightning filled the sky and the wind rattled the roof.

Gabe's wife and daughters were evacuated before the next heavy water hit, but Gabe and his son stayed in the milking parlor. They watched the water rise—the cold, black water which began to freeze their cows' lungs. Exposure set in. Then shock. The fat, complacent, gentle dairy cows that had never been bred to withstand harsh conditions, began to succumb one by one—the barn filled with their last scared moans.

Gabe wasn't an emotional man. He'd lived on farms all his life, he understood nature was cruel. He'd accepted it all. Now, however, he contemplated taking a shotgun and shooting every one of his cows so they wouldn't have to suffer the rising water. So the bawling would go away.

But Gabe didn't. Because some cows remained standing. Even as the water grew colder, the night darker, they stood. Their companions sunk around them, but some survival instinct, some need deeper than definition, kept them on their feet. If they could try, he had to let them.

He lost one hundred and twenty-six cows that night.

The rest endured. When the water finally receded, they sank into the mud, their legs shaking too hard to support them. And he and his son rubbed them down as if they were champion athletes who'd just brought home the gold.

He had one hundred cows left and twenty-eight calves. His house was ruined, his fields wouldn't be fit for at least a year. His tractor worked, but the pumps in his milking parlor had to be replaced.

"I got straw," he told Josie now, "from the last batch donated from Oregon. But there wasn't much alfalfa given out. Sly's letting me use one of his fields, but grass ain't enough for dairy. I'm gonna need forty…fifty thousand in feed to get through the winter."

"Did you go to the fairgrounds and talk to FEMA?"

"Yes, ma'am." He twisted his baseball cap nervously.

"There's all these agent people sitting around the Exhibition Hall. You gotta find the one right agency for your needs, they told me. I filled out the paperwork, but no one knew what to do with me. They asked me what I made gross—"

"Gross?"

"Yes, ma'am. And I told them two hundred thousand. So then they said I wasn't supposed to be in the farmer's line, I was supposed to be in the small business's. I went to small business's, but that man said I was a farm, not a small business, and he sent me back to the first agent. Ma'am, I got a farm to get up and running. I got a hundred head to milk twice a day. I can't keep making appointments, filling out paperwork and standing in line. It's been more than three months. The farm people finally wrote me a check for twenty thousand. That'll fix the milking parlor, buy a little feed. Then what?"

"Okay." Josie raised a hand. She understood how overwhelmed he felt, because in the beginning, she'd felt that way, too. Now, after more than three months, she'd learned how to navigate the system that was drowning him. "We have a few options."

He perked up. Most of the people she met were honest, hardworking folks, men of action. Bureaucracy and red tape killed them. Things to do made them happy.

"First, I'll take this copy of your paperwork over to FEMA and talk to them myself. It's actually net earnings that matter, which is why you were having some confusion. I can get it straightened out for you, though, no problem. However—" she skimmed his carefully recorded financials with an expert eye "—you'll probably only get ten or twenty thousand more. That won't be enough."

The tight look had reappeared around his eyes. His hands methodically twisted his hat. "No, ma'am."

"Do you have flood insurance?"

He smiled weakly. "Flood insurance for these parts? Seemed too pessimistic."

"I know, believe me, I know." Josie opened her filing cabinet and began pulling out flyers. Grand Springs hadn't had a significant flood in sixty years. Most people had been caught uninsured. She passed a small stack of papers over to Gabe, smiling when he winced. "They're not forms," she assured him, "it's information on programs for you to consider. It sounds like you've started fixing your milking parlor."

"Yes, ma'am, with the FEMA money."

"And you've been milking your cows?"

"Yes, ma'am. Sylvester has let me use his parlors for a bit. I got my cows at his place."

"So you have some income?"

"A little." He looked haggard. "But the price of milk is low, and production is down by half. The cows have been through a major trauma, ma'am. They got respiratory problems, they're weak.... It's going to take a year before they're back one hundred percent."

"If I can find you feed, Mr. Chouder, can the cows pay for their food?"

"Yes, ma'am. I think so. But that's it. The rest of the expenses..." He shook his head.

"For now, you need your herd to support itself and get strong. You'll have a rough winter, but if we can get you through, next year will be better. Has anyone talked to you about the low-interest loans available through FEMA?"

He was already shaking his hands, pushing the paper back. "No offense, ma'am, but you know how much debt I already have? I take more, and I slave for the banks for the rest of my life—or until the next disaster strikes and they foreclose on my farm. No, thank you, ma'am. I've seen too many good farmers go down that tube."

Josie understood fully. Most of the small businesses in Grand Springs were financing their way through the next year. As she'd been telling Hal time and time again, farmers just didn't have that option. They needed more ingenious solutions.

"I know of a few other programs for you to consider," she told him quietly. "First, have you heard of the Mennonite Disaster Service?"

"They're like the Amish, right? I've seen them around town. The women wear little white caps."

"That's right. They're not quite like the Amish. They use modern equipment, so to speak. Right now, we have ten Mennonite couples staying at the Boy Scout camp. They drove in to help out. They're a volunteer service, and they've been rebuilding homes and farms across the valley. In their group, they have an electrician and a plumber, so they're full service—"

"They just do this?"

"Yes." She indicated the little blue flyer. "They help those in most dire need first. The fact that you have three children and are uninsured may put you at the top of their list. You'll have to go to the camp and speak to them. If you qualify, they can probably repair your home in a matter of days and help you get your milking parlor reinstalled, as well. They're very, very good."

Gabe looked uncertain, but after a moment, he took the flyer. "At the Boy Scout camp, you say?"

"Yes, sir. Talk to them, Mr. Chouder. They're here for people like you. Someday, maybe you can return the favor by helping build somebody else's home or barn."

"All...all right."

"And the Grand Springs Farm Bureau has opened a bank account for all the donations and fund-raising moneys. A lot of that money will be used to purchase alfalfa to get through the winter. However, you can also apply to receive a small grant. We probably can't afford to give more than a few thousand per farmer, but it will give you something."

"Yes, ma'am." He wasn't enthusiastic. A few thousand barely bought a new cow, let alone got a farmer through a winter.

"Finally, I'm looking into starting an adopt-a-farm program."

"Ma'am?"

"It's been tried in a few other states, Mr. Chouder, with a fair amount of success. Basically, we would do a bio on your farm and match you up with a volunteer who would 'adopt' your farm. They would help out with the expenses, sponsor you, so to speak, for the next winter."

He shifted uncomfortably. "I don't know, ma'am. That farm has been in my family for three generations. My son's interested in it now—"

"You're not selling it, Mr. Chouder. You're not giving it away. You're just getting help to make it through the next year."

"But...but what do they get out of it?"

"The usual. The sponsor gets the satisfaction of helping someone out. Also, quite frankly, most of these people are well off and benefit from the tax deduction. They also like feeling that they're giving back to the community and helping with 'grass roots Americana.'"

Mr. Chouder was shaking his head. "Sounds too much like pity."

Josie bit the inside of her cheeks to keep from sighing. The program really could work except for one major stumbling block—farmers had phenomenal pride. It was one thing to receive help from their own, quite another to take assistance from outsiders, particularly, rich outsiders.

"It's not pity, it's community. People helping people through a rough time."

"I...I don't know. I don't want to have to call up some stranger with my bills. What if I need a new tractor? Do I have to ask permission? Does he get to pick it out? I dunno."

"Those kinds of details would have to be worked out. *I* would be perfectly willing to help you work them out. Usually, we create a straw budget for the year, the sponsor contributes his part of it up front, and you go on your merry way. Here, just take this and read it over. Think about it, Mr. Chouder. Please."

"All...all right." He took the small stack of flyers. The lines hadn't eased around his eyes. She'd given him options, but she couldn't give him answers. Those would take a long time to find as the whole community sifted through the aftermath.

"Do you have any more questions, Mr. Chouder? I'll follow up with FEMA for you as I promised."

"Thank you, ma'am. I guess I'm all set."

"You can stop by any time you like. Don't be afraid to call me with more questions."

"I'll...I'll give it all some thought, ma'am."

"Josie. You can call me Josie."

"Yes, ma'am."

She smiled. Looking at Gabe Chouder, she felt her heart break a little. His face was wind-worn and rugged, his eyes squinted from spending a lifetime staring into the sun. She'd moved to Grand Springs looking for the Gabe Chouders of the world. She'd sought goodness, she'd sought purity, she'd sought roots.

And now she knew the joy and heartache community could give. It reminded her of her parents. It reminded her of Olivia.

The sadness that swept through her was old, but still potent. She handled it as she always did. She nudged Mr. Chouder gently and gave him a large smile.

"It's going to be okay," she assured him firmly. "Grand Springs is a great community, Mr. Chouder. We're going to get through this!"

She walked him to the reception area right outside her office.

It was after five, but the waiting area was still filled with farmers and small businessmen. Her gaze picked out her new visitor immediately, however. He was taller, leaner than the rest. He rested against the wall, impeccably clad in a navy blue suit. Blond hair cut short to hide the wave. A hard jawline. Blue eyes that saw everything.

She knew who he was immediately. She'd met him two years ago, and her attention had wandered toward him ever since. He was the tall, straight-laced but broodingly handsome man who always stood across the room at social functions and studied her with piercing blue eyes. He was the man who'd actually inspired an erotic dream or two. He was the cop she avoided at all costs.

Now Detective Jack Stryker pushed away from the wall. He met her gaze.

He flashed his detective's shield.

"Josie Reynolds? Five minutes of your time, please."

It was funny, the déjà vu that swept over her these days. She looked as his badge, and once more, all she could think was *Not again.*

Two

Josie led Jack Stryker into her office because she had no other choice. His tall, rangy build quickly filled the space, not that there was much of it to begin with. Her office was comprised of one big oak desk, two chairs, an ancient computer and a whole wall of slate gray filing cabinets. Oh, and there were two scraggly vines hovering somewhere between life and death.

"I've got to do something about them," she muttered as she passed by the two plants on her way to the relative safety of her side of the desk. The office had only one tiny window, permitting very little light. The plants didn't like that. They probably weren't thrilled with her constantly forgetting to water them, either.

"Pardon?"

"Nothing."

Jack Stryker took the old black chair across from her. The chair was too low, making him double over his long body to fit. His knees stuck up comically, which she would have enjoyed more if he hadn't managed to somehow retain his dignity. His face was composed, his eyes sharp and patient, and his lips... You could tell a lot about a man from looking at his lips. Jack Stryker had very strong, firm lips.

Josie turned away. She smoothed her sensible gray skirt and wished she'd worn pants. She tugged at her pretty gray-and-pink-striped silk blouse, wishing she'd buttoned it up to her neck. Hell, a nun in a wimple would feel exposed sitting across from Jack Stryker. She had no idea what it was about him, but he unsettled her purely by existing. A cop, for God's sake. A Republican. She ought to have more pride.

No. Her hands were shaking. She was acutely aware of his gaze. And her office had grown too warm. Definite, definite tension in the room. She was an idiot.

"I'm Detective Jack Stryker—"

"I've met you before." She took her seat, and decided it was best to come out firing. "Look, in case you didn't notice, Detective, there's at least a dozen people out there waiting to speak with me. I can give you five minutes, that's it."

He leaned back, his blue gaze openly challenging. "I'm here about Olivia Stuart's murder. I would think that would take priority."

"Then, you didn't know Olivia very well, did you?"

He stiffened, clearly caught off guard by the sharp retort. Josie smiled sweetly. Round one to the con man's daughter. Hah, she'd been dealing with cops longer than this man had probably dreamed of becoming one. She wasn't some pushover and she wasn't going to be antagonized in her own office, even if the man looked way too good in a suit.

Across from her Detective Stryker stopped leaning back and his eyes narrowed. He had very blue eyes. She'd noticed them the first time they'd been introduced. The shade was bright, piercing, riveting. She was certain that from a hundred yards away a woman would still be able to feel those eyes on her. She definitely felt them on her now.

"How long did you know Olivia?"

"Two years."

"How did you meet her?"

"When I was interviewed for the position of Grand Springs treasurer."

"I thought you two were friends."

"We became friends over the course of the next few months. As the treasurer, I work very closely with the mayor. And Olivia..." Her voice grew husky with the raw emotion that even after almost four months thickened her throat. "Olivia was very kind. She showed me around, made sure I got settled. She was very generous, very...warm."

"Do you miss her?"

"Oh, yes."

"Have you ever thought of running for mayor yourself?"

Josie frowned, then shook her head, not following his line of questioning. "No."

"You seem to take your work very seriously."

"Of course."

"You were very patient with Gabe."

"How would you know?"

"I overheard."

"What do you mean, you overheard? The sound doesn't carry that easily to the reception area."

"It does if you put your ear against the door."

"You...you...*eavesdropped* on my conversation?" She didn't know whether to be outraged, amazed or impressed. She settled on outraged, hotly stabbing her finger through the air. "You had no right to do that. Isn't that illegal?"

"I was just leaning against the door," he said calmly. "There's no law against leaning against a door."

Damn, now she was impressed. She fought the feeling vehemently. "I thought you were the one they called 'Straight Arrow Stryker.' You do everything by the book, that's what I was told."

"I didn't break any law."

"You invaded my privacy! Worse, you invaded Mr. Chouder's privacy!"

"Ms. Reynolds, I would never repeat anything I overheard about Mr. Chouder's affairs. I was just trying to determine whether it would be appropriate for me to interrupt the conversation or not."

He said the words so steadily that she almost believed him. She caught herself immediately, of course. It was always a mistake to believe a cop. In their own way, they were as manipulative, conniving and Machiavellian as the people they were trying to catch.

She drew herself up to her full five feet six inches. "Detective Stryker, if I ever hear gossip about Mr. Chouder's financial affairs, I will personally hunt you down."

"And?"

She smiled sweetly. "And announce your five-thousand-dollar donation to the Grand Springs Farm Bureau relief fund, of course. I'm sure you want to help out Mr. Chouder and the other farmers like him as much as possible."

Perhaps it was only her imagination, but Stryker's clear-cut, voting Republican face seemed to ease into a small smile of appreciation. "You are good," he murmured.

"Hah, you haven't seen anything yet." Josie yanked open her center desk drawer and pulled out a bright yellow flyer.

"Band, Bingo, Bake Sale next Friday night. Ten dollars to get in, great country music, a chance at cash prizes in bingo, and maybe you can pick up a blueberry pie for your lonely bachelor nights. All proceeds go to the relief fund. I think you should buy two tickets."

"How did you know I was a bachelor?"

"Are you kidding? Ever since the day I moved here I have been regaled with stories of Mr. All-American, Jack Stryker. There are mothers with eligible daughters who do nothing but contemplate your future. Soon they'll have set up a Web site for you—your favorite foods, hobbies, likes, dislikes. Oh, that's right, no one's supposed to mention the name of your ex-wife. Let's see, Mary…Margaret…"

"Marjorie." His voice had become definitely tight.

"Marjorie. Well, no one's supposed to bring her up. So what do you say, two tickets?"

Jack Stryker blinked his eyes several times, appearing speechless. Was it the mention of his ex-wife, the fact that she knew he was a bachelor or her persistent pushing of the fund-raiser? Josie didn't care. In this preliminary battle of wills, she was finally winning. She liked winning, and these days, it didn't happen often.

"You're either the rudest person I've ever met or the absolute best strategist," Jack said at last.

"Why, thank you."

Before she could break out the champagne and celebrate her victory, however, he abruptly leaned closer, those sharp blue eyes narrowing dangerously. "But your distraction ploy's not going to work, Josie. We're not here to talk about bake sales and we're not here to talk about me. We're here to talk about you. Where are you from, Josie?"

"Hmm, now that I think about it, I'm sure your partner, Detective Richardson, and his new wife would love to go to the fund-raiser, as well. You should buy them two tickets while you're at it."

"Why did you come to Grand Springs?"

"The band is Sadie's Sunshine. Have you ever heard them? A little too much banjo for my taste, but they get your feet stomping."

"You always keep to yourself. You've worked here two years, you go to all the appropriate functions, but no one really knows you. Why is that?"

"I'm personally making lemon squares for the bake sale. They're a specialty of mine. Better yet, Mrs. Simone is selling a pie-a-month club. For fifty bucks, she'll deliver a fresh-baked pie to your house each month. She starts with her strawberry rhubarb pie in October. I'd buy that deal for myself, but I'm not sure I'm getting enough time at the gym for a pie a month."

"Is it men you don't like? Or cops? Or both?" His blue

eyes remained steady, his lips set. She could babble on till doomsday, his gaze told her, he would still get the information he required. As she watched him, the right corner of his lip curved dryly. "Come on, Josie," he commanded firmly. "Speak to me."

She had to look away. The nervousness started in her belly and worked its way up to her throat. She had nothing to be nervous about, she told herself again and again but it wasn't working. Her mouth had gone dry. Beneath the desk, her hands were trembling.

Dammit, she wasn't ready for this kind of interrogation. She was tired and overworked. She missed Olivia, she wanted to help Olivia, and yes, she did not like cops. Not even the one nicknamed "Straight Arrow Stryker," who she always noticed, even in a crowded room.

"Look," Josie said, "as much fun as this has been, I still have a whole reception area filled with people who have much more important questions than what's my sign. This meeting is over."

"I'm trying to solve a murder—"

"And I hope you do." Abruptly, her temper flared. She slapped her desk, startling them both. "Dammit, Olivia was my best friend! I want you to catch who killed her as much as anyone, you narrow-minded bureaucrat. And I'm telling you, I don't have any more information for you!"

"I think you're lying," he said bluntly.

"I think you've inhaled too much red ink! I think you guys are desperate for answers over there. I bet Hal's having a field day whipping your backs. Oh, and the police department's budget is up for review. I should've known."

Stryker stood so fast, his chair tipped back. His jaw was tight enough to crack three walnuts, and his eyes seemed to blaze out of his head. He was angry, she realized with awe. Not just angry. The famous Straight Arrow Stryker was furious. And God, was he magnificent!

"Don't you ever, ever accuse me or my partner of man-

ufacturing answers just to please a sniveling idiot like Hal
Stuart. I don't know how you do your job, lady, but I take
mine very seriously!''

''And so do I!''

''You're a suspect, Josie Reynolds.''

''Because I was Olivia's *friend?*''

''Because you're hiding something.'' Jack Stryker
planted his hands on her desk. He leaned all the way across
until she could feel the whisper of his breath on her cheek,
and said, ''I'm going to come back to this office, Ms.
Reynolds, and I'm going to keep coming back until I know
everything about you. Where you were, what you've done.
Why you don't like cops. And if you killed Olivia Stuart,
I'll personally slap the handcuffs on your tender wrists.''

Her mouth had gone dry. His determination was so pure,
she could almost hear the cell doors clanging shut behind
her. Again. Again. *Again.* Josie drew back slowly. She
pulled herself together and pasted a smile on her pale face,
because that's what she did best. That is what her father
had taught her.

''Does that mean you don't want four tickets to the
Band, Bingo, Bake Sale fund-raiser?''

''What?''

''I said, does that mean you don't want four tickets to
the Band, Bingo, Bake Sale fund-raiser? It's next Friday,
remember? Seven o'clock, and the money goes to—''

''Yeah, yeah, yeah,'' he raised a silencing hand, frowning deeply, studying her again as if she were a puzzle he
ought to be able to solve.

She looked him in the eye. It was the most she could
do when her stomach had fallen away, leaving her hollow
and lost. ''I take my job seriously, too, Detective. And
right now, my job means I need to raise money for those
people sitting out there wondering why a Grand Springs
detective is yelling at the Grand Springs treasurer.''

''I did not yell,'' he said immediately..

"You yelled."

"I don't yell."

"Would you like me to open the door and ask?"

Jack clutched his temples. For a moment, he definitely looked on the verge of strangling her and even he seemed surprised by the intensity of his reaction. "I'm losing my mind," she heard him mutter. "I have to get more sleep."

For the first time, Josie noticed the shadows beneath his eyes, the red tinge of his bloodshot eyes. Olivia had always spoken very highly of Jack Stryker, of his phenomenal work ethic, of his passion for his job. He was the cop who always got his man.

Until the Olivia Stuart case. For a moment, the humor of the situation struck her. Two of Grand Springs's most overworked public servants, going after each other like small children. And the sadness struck her again. Grand Springs's two lost public servants, each wanting justice for Olivia and yelling petty insults at each other instead.

"Two tickets," she said more gently. "Sounds like you could use a night off."

He grunted, which was probably his version of agreement.

"I'll take four," he said suddenly. "Stone and Jessie might as well drool over each other in public for a good cause. Are you going?"

"Yes."

"With anyone?"

Josie shook her head in frustration. "None of your business. Go home, Detective. It's almost six o'clock and I still have a lot of work to do. Try not to arrest any of the good citizens in my office on your way out."

"This isn't over."

"Oh, famous last words. Cops have absolutely no imagination."

Jack arched a brow. Far from retreating, he said somberly, "Yes, we do." He leaned over her desk.

"I'll see you at the fund-raiser, Josie. And I'll see you going home every night and I'll see you jogging every morning. I want Olivia Stuart's killer. Think about that, Josie. Think about that real hard."

He stepped out of her office. She struggled to inhale long after the door had shut behind him.

I'm not the killer, dammit. A Reynolds isn't the killer.

At nine o'clock, she turned away the last person. She hated doing that, hated seeing the stress in each person's eyes as she stood in the waiting room and softly promised to meet with them first thing in the morning. Four people were left. They'd waited six hours and now had to return tomorrow.

Goaded by guilt, she spent another two hours trying to catch up with paperwork. By eleven, her stomach was growling too much to concentrate. She cleaned up her desk, updated her list of things to do for the morning and prepared to leave. Halfway out the door she remembered she'd forgotten to speak to FEMA for Gabe Chouder.

"Damn," she muttered. "Get it on the list."

Heading back out, she remembered she'd forgotten the report on strip mining for Hal Stuart. She went back to add that to the list. The third time, she recalled her promise to speak with Helen Hunter about the bingo prizes. The fourth time, she made it through the door, stomach growling, eyes tired.

Her low-slung heels echoed in the vaulted hallways of City Hall. All the offices were dark, only the yellow ceiling lights guided her way. It was a strange, lonely feeling to be in a big marble building all alone at night. She nodded goodbye to the security guard stationed by the front doors and let herself out.

The night was cold and clear. Her car was around back. These days she wondered how safe it was to walk to her car alone, but still had no choice. At least, she encountered no surprises tonight.

She drove home on deserted roads and pulled up to a dark one-story rancher. She had no roommates, no pets, no people to help her, which meant she got to drag the garbage can to the curb even though she didn't feel like doing it. Monday was garbage night, so out it went.

Back inside, she snapped on the kitchen light and set her briefcase and jacket on the kitchen table. She was spending too much time at work, and her small house showed it. Plants drooped from lack of water. The simple, sparse furniture had gathered a thick layer of dust. Abruptly, the whole place depressed her. She had a house, but not a home. A home shouldn't smell as alien and stale as her place did now.

She stared at the brown kitchen cabinets and contemplated heating up a can of soup. Food might make her feel better. When a person burned the candle at both ends, food and nutrition became even more important, she reminded herself. But the act of taking out a saucepan and opening a can sounded like too much work. Did a man like Stryker come home to an empty house, as well? Did he contemplate heating up soup and realize he was too tired, or did a man as handsome as him have a new woman every night, happy to fill the void?

She could still remember the tight feeling in her belly when Grand Springs's most eligible bachelor had pinned her with his gaze. And she recalled the secret, nearly primal thrill of making ''Straight Arrow Stryker'' yell.

Oh God, what was she thinking? She gave up on cooking, dropped her clothes on the floor, and climbed into bed.

Her dreams brought her comfort. She was ten years old again. She knew because her blond hair was in the kind of beautiful French braid only her mother could do. She sat at the simple kitchen table. Her mom was making cookies and the kitchen smelled of nutmeg and vanilla.

The back door opened as her father walked in, wearing a suit he'd donned first thing in the morning and now accessorized it with his hearty smile. Her mom looked up, her eyes immediately going soft. Rose's gaze always went tender when she saw Stan.

"I got me a job, Rose. Selling cars. I'm going straight, just like I promised."

"Oh, Stan. Thank you. Thank you so much."

He wrapped her pretty mama in a big bear hug. In his suit, he looked big and handsome, all red hair and snapping blue eyes. In her spring dress, her mother was his perfect complement, all blond hair and delicately defined features.

Her mother sat Stan at the table. He got his own plate with four oatmeal cookies, sneaking one to Josie when Rose turned for the milk. She palmed it effortlessly, the way he'd taught her, and he winked at her until she giggled.

Josie was the luckiest girl in the world and she knew it. She was Stan's little girl, and Stan was the only father on the block who knew how to make dreams come true. And when Rose smiled at Stan the way Rose was smiling at Stan now, there wasn't anything Stan couldn't do.

Josie inhaled the scents of nutmeg and vanilla. She let the oatmeal cookie melt on her tongue.

"I want to stay here always, Daddy," she whispered in her sleep.

"Of course you can," he promised her in her dream. "Of course you can."

Her alarm clock went off at six. She awoke disoriented and groggy. She sat up with a scowl, impatiently pushing a cloud of tangled hair out of her face.

"Liar," she muttered. Her room, empty and still dark gray with morning, didn't argue. She pattered into her bathroom and buried herself beneath the scouring spray of a hot shower.

* * *

"Well, I'm so happy you finally found time for your family!"

Jack leaned over and kissed his mother's cheek. "Nice to see you, too, Mom."

He shook his father's hand as the older man apologized for Betty Stryker's comment with his gaze. Jack understood. His mother was a high-strung, anxious woman. Sometimes she was on medication, but mostly she tried to manage it on her own. It wasn't easy. Betty Stryker's world was filled with demons and worry. And the death of her oldest son at the age of eighteen had only made the shadows darker.

"We're grilling steaks," Betty announced. She stood in the middle of the simple living room, nicely attired in chocolate-colored slacks and an off-white turtleneck. She twisted each ring on her right hand in turn and then started over again.

"Steak sounds great," Jack told her.

"Are you sure? I have chicken I could defrost. We still have some of that salmon in the freezer...."

"Steak is perfect. Honest. Crazy as things have been lately, a nice thick steak sounds wonderful."

"Are you working too hard? How is Hal Stuart as acting mayor? I heard he's a real tyrant. Is he too demanding? Are you getting enough sleep?"

Ben took his wife's arm and led her toward the kitchen. "Jack is doing just fine, dear. Policemen don't expect regular hours, do they?"

"Work's not bad at all," Jack agreed, when in fact both he and his father knew he hadn't slept for more than six hours a night in months. "Can I help you with anything?"

"No, no. Just sit right down at the table. I'll get the salad. Ben, will you check the steaks on the grill?"

His mother bustled around. Movement helped keep the restlessness down. Jack sat down at the table in the same seat he'd occupied since his parents had moved into the house when he was four. It was a simple three-bedroom rancher made of good, solid construction. His father had earned enough as an electrician to support the whole family. They'd been comfortable growing up, but never rich. Family vacations were generally camping in the mountains, not flying to Disneyland.

Jack had been happy, though. Ben had taught him and Tom how to hunt and track. There had been weekends fishing together, then the Boy Scouts. Tom had ridiculed the Boy Scouts after the first three years. Jack had continued on to become an Eagle Scout, however, while his father became a troop leader. Right after Tom's death, when emotions were still too high for words, Jack and his father had gone on the Scout trips together and let the hiking sweat the pain from their pores. By nightfall, they could sit together in front of the campfire, watching the flickering flames and finding comfort in just being there, side by side, father and son, bonded by the silence.

Jack wondered if such things would've helped his mother. Instead, she always stayed home, shutting herself up in the house where Tom's room became a museum to an eighteen-year-old rebel, each item still exactly where Tom had placed it nearly twenty years ago. Even now, sitting at the table, the fourth chair carried a full weight of silent accusation and guilt.

I am Tom's chair. Don't you remember him sitting here, throwing peas at you across the table and laughing the way only Tom could laugh? Don't forget, don't forget.

Betty returned with the salad. Ben followed her with the steaks. Corn on the cob, freshly steamed and rich with butter, already sat in the middle. Betty poured two glasses of milk for Jack and his father, then a glass of water for herself. Her gaze darted briefly to Tom's chair before she sat.

They began the meal in silence, the way they always did.

"Have either of you seen Paige Summers," his mother said at last, her voice slightly high-pitched, as if she was seeking to fill all the silent voids in their lives. "I ran into her at the grocery store just the other day. I would swear she was pregnant."

"Haven't seen her," Jack confessed.

"I didn't think she had a boyfriend," Betty pressed. "I haven't heard of any boyfriend and she certainly isn't married. Last I knew, she was just starting out as a secretary for Jared Montgomery's real estate firm. Imagine. This town just isn't what it used to be."

"It's none of our business," Jack said quietly. He'd met Paige Summers only once, but she seemed like a genuinely nice, sweet woman. If she was single and pregnant, then she had enough to deal with and didn't need any undue gossip. He finished eating his salad. His father dished up the steaks. After a bit, Jack found himself asking, "Do either of you know Josie Reynolds?"

"She's the town treasurer," Betty said promptly. She prided herself on knowing who was who in the community.

"You ever met her?"

"I saw her at the Jamesons' Christmas party last year. Oh, that blond hair of hers. Just gorgeous. You wouldn't know she was an accountant to look at her."

Jack agreed with that. He looked at his father, who was nodding.

"She's good," Ben said. "A real hard worker."

Jack raised a brow. That was high praise coming from Ben, who'd worked sixty hours a week all his life to support his family, plus volunteered as a community fireman and Scout leader. "Why do you say that?"

"I've been working with her."

"You have?"

"Sure, I've been helping out with the fund-raisers. You know the community auction two weeks ago? Josie's idea. She's even the one who called the companies and got them to donate the computers and plane tickets. We raised fifteen thousand dollars that night."

"I didn't know that."

"The big dinner and theater at the old mill? Josie's idea. She got Grand Springs's community theater to volunteer their play, and Touch of Class Catering to provide all the food at cost. Made two thousand off of that."

"Oh."

"Then this Friday we've got the Band, Bingo, Bake Sale coming up—"

"That I know about. In fact, I bought four tickets."

"Good, good." His father nodded approvingly. "Josie's idea again. Sadie's Sunshine called her up and said they'd like to do something to help out, and Josie set it all up. Smart woman. She really pitches in. People like her."

"Who are you taking to the bake sale, dear?" his mother asked. She wasn't too interested in the fund-raisers. Organizing activities taxed her nerves.

"Uh…I haven't really thought about it." Jack quickly turned back to his father. When his mother got on this topic, it took a hurricane to shake her off. "So you've talked to Josie a few times?"

"Oh, yeah, I work with her a lot." His father was very active in the community.

"Has she ever mentioned where she's from?"

"No."

"What about her family? Does she talk about family?"

"No."

"Are you going to take Josie to the bake sale?"

"No," Jack said to his mother with probably more force than necessary. "I'm just…I'm just curious, that's all." He didn't bring up her tie to the Olivia Stuart case. He made it a point never to talk about his job in front of his mother. He was still frowning, however. He couldn't get the mystery of Josie Reynolds out of his mind. "Don't you find it odd that she never talks about her personal life?" he persisted. "She's hardly a quiet woman. She's definitely not shy," he muttered.

His father chuckled. "She has spirit. You should hear her with the FEMA folks. That's kinda fun."

"But Dad—"

Ben shrugged. "She likes her privacy, Jack. She's got a right."

"She's very beautiful," his mother said. "And unattached."

"I'm not interested in her that way, Mom. Really, I don't have time right now to be interested in anyone. I like my life the way it is."

His parents exchanged a look he'd seen too many times before. He abruptly set down his silverware. "Is it true everyone's afraid to mention Marjorie's name when I'm around?"

Betty's eyes widened. She looked at Ben for help.

"Well, Jack," he began in a careful, placating tone.

"Oh, God, it is true. It's been five years, Dad. I can handle it."

"She wasn't right for you," his mother said immediately. "I told you from the beginning that she wasn't right. Anyone could tell just by looking at her that she had the morals of an alley cat."

Jack winced and pushed away his plate. He'd lied, after all. "I don't want to talk about it."

His parents exchanged that look again. His ex-wife Marjorie had been a faithless bitch, there was no other word for it. She was the only mistake Jack had ever made, but boy, had it been a big one. He was the type of man who'd assumed he would marry only once. He would meet the perfect, kind, beautiful woman and be faithful forever. They'd raise two children, eat dinner together every night and hike on the weekends. Hell, maybe the dreams had been too Ozzie and Harriet for the nineties. Certainly, coming home early and finding his beautiful wife in bed with a muscle-bound rookie officer hadn't been among his plans. Nor had he ever imagined the way she'd looked him right in the eye and said, "You deserved this Jack. You never could give me what I need."

The fancy town house, the luxury automobile, the role of the future mayor's wife.

Jack was good at many things, but he wasn't good at forgiving, and he never quite forgot.

"How about some after-dinner coffee?" his mother asked brightly. "Or would you like tea? I have jasmine, mint, English breakfast and chamomile. Or maybe you'd like some cognac, I think your father has cognac. Don't you have cognac, Ben?"

"Coffee would be perfect, Mom. Here, why don't you sit for a change and let me help you."

"Oh, no, no. You just stay right there. I know where everything is, it will only be a minute. It's not every day you come to see us. The least I can do is brew you some coffee."

Jack watched her bustle away, her movements nervous and jerky. When she pulled out the coffeepot it shook in her hands.

"It's all right," Ben said softly beside him. "The blackout was tough for her, but she's doing pretty well these days. Sleeping through the nights."

"That's good."

"It has been five years since…since that woman," Ben said abruptly. He always referred to Marjorie as simply "that woman." "You made a mistake marrying her, Jack, but that's all right. You were young and she was beautiful and had that effect on men. Now, Josie Reynolds… Mark my words, Jack, she's special. Tough as nails, works harder than a dog and beautiful from the inside out. She's who you need. A girl like that will really challenge you. Take her to the fund-raiser. Give dating a chance.''

"Not you, too, Dad," Jack groaned.

"On some things, your mother is right.''

Betty returned. She handed out the cups of coffee, then passed around the cream and sugar. They drank the coffee in silence, and as always, Betty's gaze was on Tom's chair.

Three

Jack spent the next three days getting back to basics. He'd gotten a degree in criminology because it appealed to his methodical mind. Police work wasn't sexy and it wasn't instinctive. It was science. First you studied the crime scene, looking at MO, weapon and trace evidence. Then you analyzed the area where the crime took place—what kind of economics and demographics? Were you looking at a high-crime area or low-crime area? Was it racially homogenous or mixed? Then you did a profile of the victim. Was it a low-risk victim or a high-risk victim? Known friends, known enemies, major events going on in her life? Finally, you boiled all that information down, and if all went well, you had a list of potential suspects to interrogate. You got to go hunting.

The crime scene gave them nothing: no hair, no fiber, no prints, no weapon. The storm had obscured any footprints that may have been. Nothing had been stolen or disturbed. The area—upper class, white, suburban—told them only that their suspect was probably white and well-groomed, otherwise, someone would've noticed him or her. In Grand Springs, however, white, middle-class suburbanites were a dime a dozen. Olivia's neighborhood was quiet and safe, not the kind of place where random murders just happened.

In short, Olivia's murder had not been about theft. It had not been gang-related nor drug-related. It had been personal. It had been planned by someone sophisticated enough to know about pure potassium and how to inject it into a strong, healthy woman.

Jack pursued the only other option he had left—he focused on the victim, Olivia.

In the course of three days, he retraced her last twenty-four hours and the people and events influenced along the way. It took a while. Olivia had been a very active woman.

On June 5, her day began with an 8:00 a.m. meeting with her personal secretary, the school board, and a representative from D.A.R.E. talking about starting an anti-drug program in the high school. At nine, Olivia had left for a general meeting with the city council. The minutes revealed that they'd focused primarily on the issue of strip mining. That meeting had overrun half an hour due to heated debate. According to attendees, Olivia had remained steadfastly opposed to strip mining, tabling the initiative.

Now running late, Olivia had barely made it to the Chamber of Commerce luncheon in time to speak. She'd finished there at one and driven straight to the women's shelter, where she'd spent an hour playing with the children and talking to the mothers. According to Denise Eagan, head of the shelter, Olivia tried to spend at least an hour a week at the shelter. They had been talking about the possibility of opening a second to get more beds. Olivia had promised to speak to the city council about funding.

At three o'clock Olivia had returned to her office. She'd spent two hours on the phone. Her secretary didn't have information on all the calls, but according to the phone records most of them were to various businesses and local charities. She'd made one call to her home, where her daughter, Eve, and five-year-old granddaughter, Molly, were visiting for Hal's wedding.

Olivia had rushed out of the office promptly at five-thirty, changed into a pale lavender suit, and made it to the Squaw Creek Lodge just in time for the wedding rehearsal. Afterward, the wedding party had gone out for dinner. Olivia had toasted her son and his intended bride, Randi Howell. Eve said Olivia had looked tired from her day, but otherwise her mother had been as calm and composed as ever. She'd told jokes, she'd mingled with Randi's family.

Eve hadn't noticed anything unusual.

They'd retired right after dinner. Everyone wanted to get a good night's sleep before the big day. Friday morning Olivia had gotten up early with Eve and Molly. Olivia and Molly had just finished eating cereal when Eve came downstairs. They'd talked some, about nothing in particular. Olivia had said how nice it was to have Eve at home again. She'd thought Molly was growing up fast and beautiful. Eve could tell her mother was wondering if Eve would ever tell Rio Redtree that Molly was his daughter, but on Friday June 6, Olivia kept those opinions to herself.

She and Eve had wrapped wedding presents, cleaned the house in preparation for guests and then they'd gotten ready to go. At the last minute, still searching for her other earring, Olivia had told Eve to take Molly and go ahead. She'd be there shortly. The storm was already moving in at that point. The rain and wind had picked up. They'd both remarked how unfortunate it was that the weather couldn't be better for the wedding.

Eve had bundled up Molly and the two of them had left.

Eve never saw Olivia alive again.

Jack went over it and over it. He was beginning to dream about Olivia Stuart's life at night. He still couldn't figure out what they were missing.

For all intents and purposes, Olivia Stuart had been an active mayor and caring mother. Her calendar and meetings showed nothing out of the ordinary. She was definitely concerned about Grand Springs's growing drug problem and crime rate. Her schedule for the next week had two meetings with community watch groups and one with the chief of police. Olivia's secretary confirmed that Olivia had wanted Grand Springs to get tougher about crime, but she hadn't had any run-ins with any particular criminal group.

The only other big issue was strip mining. The outlying areas of Grand Springs sat on top of what once had been very lucrative mines. Now mined out, they were just hollow tunnels forming catacombs beneath the mountain and potential safety hazards. The local kids hung out there— Jack spent most of his youth learning which mines could be explored and which ones should be left alone. Recently, one of the big mining companies had approached Grand Springs about the possibility of renewing the old mining leases so as to harvest the remaining minerals and ore in the top soil through strip mining.

If permitted, the project would generate hundreds of jobs for Grand Springs and boost the economy. As Olivia passionately argued, however, it would also tax the city's mountain roads and lead to such possible consequences as top soil erosion, mud slides, contaminated rivers and air pollution.

Olivia had said no. Her stance was firm and there were definitely businesspeople who disagreed with her. But would any of them resort to murder?

Jack didn't think so.

The more he looked at Olivia Stuart's life, the more he thought the answers had nothing to do with her position as mayor. Olivia Stuart was a cautious woman. Eve reported that the house was kept locked at all times, even when Olivia was home. The mayor had attended a number of self-defense classes and insisted the security guard at City Hall walk all female employees to their cars after dark.

Yet there was no sign of forced entrance into her home

nor any indication of a struggle. The back door had been unlocked when Josie Reynolds had arrived.

A lone woman didn't just open her door for anyone on a stormy afternoon. And the use of poison...

Jack kept coming back to the same inevitable conclusion: Olivia Stuart had been killed by someone she knew. Someone she trusted.

And it bothered Jack that he couldn't learn more about Olivia's private life. Eve was as vague as Hal. She'd been away from home for five years. She spoke to Olivia by phone, of course, but she couldn't remember Olivia ever talking about anyone new or special. Olivia hadn't seemed to have any problems with her friends or associates. As for romantic interests, Eve agreed with her brother—Olivia didn't date.

Their father had died in an accident when Eve was only a toddler and Hal ten. They'd had an older brother, Roy, but he'd run away and never been heard from again. As Eve told Jack proudly, Olivia had decided it was time to get control of her life and take a stand. She'd thrown herself into supporting Hal and Eve, going back to school, becoming a lawyer and eventually running for mayor. She'd become a single mother and a career woman at a time when those things just weren't done, and she'd been good at it. If Olivia had made enemies, she kept them as secret as the rest of the details of her life.

The only lead Jack had left was Josie Reynolds. She'd been close to Olivia. She matched the vague description of the woman Jessie had seen in her visions. She could be called Jo.

At 9:00 p.m. Thursday, Jack told himself he was just taking a small detour when he went by Josie's house. All the windows were dark. He didn't bother to lie to himself when he turned around and headed for City Hall.

The light was on up in her office. He sat in his car for a minute, simply staring at the single lit window. Everyone agreed on two things about Josie Reynolds—she looked like an angel and worked like the Energizer bunny.

Conscientious public servant?

Ambitious treasurer, now angling for the empty position of mayor?

Marjorie certainly would've plotted on becoming mayor.

The thought came out of nowhere and unsettled Jack. He was an honest enough man that he didn't want to think he was placing Marjorie's crimes on Josie's doorstep. On the other hand, maybe the instinct was sound.

Or maybe you're not as objective as you think when it comes to Josie Reynolds.

Jack got out of his car, took a deep breath and prepared for round two.

Josie was so deeply engrossed in her work, she didn't hear the sound of footsteps ringing in the empty hall. The knock on her door got her attention. She bolted up and smeared a line of red ink across the report she'd been editing.

"Damn." She stared at her door mutinously. It was after nine o'clock. What did a girl have to do to get some peace and quiet around here? Then she got nervous. Exactly who would be knocking on the town treasurer's door at this hour?

"Mr. Stevens?" she called out, referring to the aging security guard who'd started work last month. She'd never seen him stand, much less walk, but maybe his hemorrhoids had flared up or something.

"It's Detective Stryker."

"Oh," she said, then with more feeling, "damn."

She eyed the door warily—why did some part of her perk up at the sound of his voice?—then grudgingly threw open the door. She didn't look her best and she knew it. It was after hours, she'd had a long day, and a woman could handle only so much. She'd taken off her navy blue double-breasted jacket at five, her heels quickly following. She'd sneaked into the ladies' room and removed her nylons at six. When the last person had left at eight-thirty, she'd pulled out her white blouse from her skirt, unfastened the cuffs and high collar and pulled the hairpins from her hair. Now at approximately 9:35 p.m., she was a mussed, wrinkled mess and she refused to feel bad about it.

Of course, Jack Stryker leaned against the doorjamb without a short-cropped hair out of place. His charcoal gray suit was pressed razor-sharp and did his tall, trim figure justice. He wore an appropriately conservative yet elegant dark burgundy-and-gray swirled tie.

Oh for crying out loud her mouth had gone dry. Since when did Josie Reynolds get hot and bothered by a wool suit?

"Can I come in?" Jack asked.

She pursed her lips. "I haven't decided."

"I have a badge."

"Why do you think I can't decide?" She crossed her arms over her silk blouse. That made the unbuttoned collar gape, revealing a weakness for expensive French lingerie no accountant should have. She dropped her hands quickly to her side, but it was too late. Jack's gaze was definitely no longer on her face, and his cheeks appeared to have gained some color. "Don't you have some teenage delinquents to torture?" she demanded with a scowl.

"I'm a homicide detective. I only get to deal with gang members who have close encounters with assault weapons."

"Well, I'm a treasurer. I only get to deal with credits and debits, so go away and let me get my job done."

"Tough day at the office?" He arched a brow.

"Yes," she fired back. Her hands had come up on her hips. She said with genuine regret, "My plants died."

"Your plants died?"

"The two vines over on the gray filing cabinet?" He still looked blank. She shook her head. "Why am I bothering with this conversation? You're a man. Men never notice anything, not even homicide detectives."

"Wait a second." Now she'd gotten his goat. It occurred to her that she'd been trying to all along. All women needed a form of entertainment. "I remember those two plants," Jack said with a frown, "They were already dead."

"No. They were in critical condition. But with the right amount of water, sunlight and care, they would've sprung back. Of course, they're trapped in a dimly lit office with a woman who's trying to repair flood damage. Have you ever noticed that the more you talk about floods, the harder it is to even drink a glass of water? I find myself staring at it like it's the enemy, just waiting for my guard to drop."

"You have been working too hard," Jack said seriously.

"Absolutely. So go away, I don't need any more interruptions in my day."

"I can't."

"Yes, you can. You just turn around, walk down the hall and nod at Stevens as you exit the building. You strike me as a former Boy Scout—"

"Eagle Scout."

"Eagle Scout? Of course." Now her tone was dry. She waved her fingers at him. "So you ought to be able to find your way just about anywhere without getting lost. Toodle-oo."

She reached for her office door, he blocked her move with his arm. Damn. Her belly had gone tight, she felt almost giddy. Oh, they were dueling all right, but behind the words lurked a more dangerous game. The temperature of the room had definitely racheted up a few degrees.

"I need to talk to you." Jack stated.

"Detective, no offense, but I'm working way too many hours to put up with you, as well. It's almost ten o'clock. I still have to finish this report. I haven't even eaten lunch. If my stomach growls any louder, you could arrest me for disturbing the peace. Please, go away. Make an appointment if you have to come back. Better yet, make dinner reservations."

"All right."

"What?"

"You haven't eaten, I haven't eaten. I am going to ask you questions. Now, I can stand in your doorway for the event, or, if you'd like, we could go get a bite to eat."

"I...I..." Josie stared down at her wrinkled silk blouse and creased navy blue skirt. Her bare feet, with their red-painted toenails, stared back at her. She'd forgotten about her toenails. Her whole body abruptly flushed with mortification. She was too exposed. "Tomorrow night," she said weakly. "I'm...I'm not dressed for it now."

"Tomorrow night's the fund-raiser. I thought you were going." He added dryly, "I have four tickets."

Now her cheeks were definitely hot red. "I'm not dressed to go out now."

"We'll go someplace casual."

"No. No, really, I'm not hungry anymore." Her stomach growled loudly and endlessly. She stared at the ceiling and pretended the noise had come from the vents. Jack, of course, was amused. The smug son of a...

"You don't have to order anything," he said with feigned innocence. "You can watch the glasses of water in case they're planning a fresh attack."

"That's not funny."

"Josie, I've had a long week as well. Now, come with me or I'll throw you over my shoulder and personally carry you to the restaurant."

"Police brutality!"

"Necessary use of force. Want to grab your purse now? My stomach's about to growl, too."

She scowled harder. She didn't trust Jack Stryker. Most of the time she was pretty sure she didn't like him. Worse, she was even more certain that she liked him too much. There was a good reason they had been avoiding each other for two years. And now?

"I'm buying my own dinner," she said stiffly. "I don't accept free meals from cops—there are too many strings attached."

"Fine. Don't you think you should put on your shoes, as well?"

"Oh." She fought back another blush and recovered her heels from beneath her desk with as much dignity as possible.

Jack took her to a corner diner, the kind of place frequented by cops and people working night shifts. The pink Formica tabletops were sticky, and the red vinyl booths patched with gray duct tape. A gum-cracking waitress tossed laminated menus at them, poured two cups of thick coffee without asking and walked away.

Josie stared after her with open admiration. "Now, that's attitude."

"Wait till she returns to take our order. You'll discover the menus are just for show. They serve whatever the cook feels like making that particular evening."

"I see. Come here often?"

"Often enough. The coffee is strong and the food good." He set down his menu and folded his hands on the edge of the table, looking at her intently.

She returned his gaze inch for inch, her chin stubbornly in the air.

Jack, however, didn't speak right away. Instead, his eyes took on the dim stare of a man whose mind was already a million miles away. Was he thinking about the case? Or maybe this evil ex-wife she'd heard rumors about. Mary…Margaret…Marjorie. The evil Marjorie.

She scrutinized him, trying to get some insight into his cool, controlled expression. The lights in the diner were harsh and far from kind. This close, she could see the fresh lines around his eyes and the pall of sleepless nights tingeing his skin. He was ragged around the edges, as if life was beating him up a bit. She knew that feeling.

"You don't have any leads, do you," she asked bluntly.

He didn't bother to pretend. "Just you."

"Me?"

"We know it's a woman with blond hair and the nickname Jo. How many people call you Jo, Josie?"

"That's…that's ridiculous!" she exclaimed, but she was shaken. They were looking for a blond woman named Jo? She hadn't known that. Suddenly, she didn't feel so well. "No one calls me Jo," she tried to protest. She was lying. Her father had called her Jo. When she'd been really young and her hair cut short, he would dress her up as his son Joe, depending on the scam they were running.

"Everyone has a nickname."

"How do you know it's a woman?"

"I'm not at liberty to discuss that."

"Oh, well, I beg your pardon! You're at liberty to accuse me, but not tell me why. Must be great to be a cop!" There was too much anger in that last sentence and they both knew it.

"You seem to have a thing against the police, Josie. Why is that?"

"I'm head of the Save-the-Doughnuts Foundation," she said flippantly. "Can't you people see the damage you're inflicting on pastries everywhere?"

"Cute. Want to try again?"

"No, I don't. I'm not 'at liberty to say.' Now, are you going to feed me, or was that just a ruse to get me in heels before you cut me down to size?"

"We can order." His tone was controlled and dispassionate. She sat across from him and silently contemplated his death. It hurt her that he could be so distant. It hurt her that he was the quintessential cop when a part of her had wanted him to be something more. Someone worthy of the secret tingles he sometimes sent up her spine. Well, she was stupid.

The waitress arrived. As Jack had predicted, most items on the menu were currently unavailable. However, they could order turkey with trimmings or roast beef. They both ordered the turkey.

Josie got milk and sugar for her coffee and doctored it up. Even then, the first sip made her eyes pop open. "Wah! That could put hair on your chest."

"Brewed all day for that special punch."

"Yes, indigestion."

They lapsed into awkward silence.

"So you're going to the fund-raiser tomorrow night?" Jack asked at last.

"Yes. And you?"

"Definitely. Stone and Jessica are coming, as well."

"What are you doing with the fourth ticket?"

"My dad."

"Ben?" She brightened. "You have a wonderful father, Jack. He works so hard! Did you know he's helped rewire some of the farms and businesses? He's such a generous man."

"He mentioned that he was helping out," Jack said neutrally. Mention of his father had definitely put a spark in Josie's eyes. Something tightened his gut. It was suspiciously close to jealousy.

Josie was stirring her coffee again. Her movements were brisk and energetic. She'd appeared tired and disgruntled when he'd first arrived at her office; the strain around her eyes was genuine. But now she was catching her second wind. A delicate color tinged her cheeks and brightened her blue eyes. Her pale blond hair glowed soft and flaxen down around her shoulders. She still hadn't buttoned her silk blouse, and when she leaned forward, he had a glimpse of frothy lace and creamy skin. She wasn't a tall woman, or a large woman. But she carried herself with a definite energetic presence that took some getting used to. It wasn't his mother's nervous restlessness, it was genuine vitality. And he found it unbelievably attractive.

He really needed to get more sleep.

She spoke. He watched her tongue moisten her pale, pink lips, then saw them move.

"What?" he asked belatedly, realizing he'd just missed everything.

"I asked how your mother is. Ben mentioned last week that she was feeling 'under the weather.'"

"My mom?" Jack frowned. He didn't want to discuss his mother. He twirled his coffee mug with his fingers, almost burning himself as the hot liquid sloshed over the side. "My mom isn't sick in the traditional sense, if that's what you mean. She's…she's, uh, a little high-strung. Anxious, nervous. She gets a lot of migraine headaches."

"Oh." Josie sounded genuinely surprised, then sympathetic. "June must have been very difficult for her."

"It was, but she got through. She does try very hard. Life just isn't as easy for her as it is for others."

"I'm sorry to hear that."

"Don't be. It has nothing to do with you."

"Your job is hard for her, isn't it? If she worries all the time, having a cop in the family would be tough."

"Yes."

"But you did it, anyway."

"It's the only thing I ever wanted to be."

"Oh." For a moment, she sounded contrite.

Jack pushed away his coffee mug. "Besides, Grand Springs is hardly a big city. When I joined the force, we hadn't had an officer seriously injured in the line of duty in years. These days… Well, things are changing, but I'm not about to give up my job just when it's needed most."

"Everyone in the world is moving to small towns to get away from crime," Josie said with a sigh. "And instead, crime just follows us."

"Grand Springs isn't a small town anymore."

"No, but it would be nice if the culture stayed that way."

"It has. Folks are a lot nicer to one another here than in big cities. We still help one another out. You've been involved in the fund-raisers, you ought to know that as well as anyone."

"True, the flood has really pulled the community together. People like your father have helped make a huge difference. Do you know how incredible it was the week after the flood? After the *Grand Springs Herald* carried the first story on the damage, the response was amazing. The phone in my office rang off the hook with people wanting to know what they could do to help. We had six-year-olds bringing in their piggy banks, housewives mailing in grocery money. Plumbers, electricians and carpenters all donated their time to help rebuild. From all over the state, all over the country, we received donations and offers of assistance. Floods and mud slides make you respect the power of Mother Nature. The cleanup afterward makes you respect the power of community."

"Absolutely."

The waitress arrived with two plates of turkey, stuffing and cranberry sauce. Both of them picked up their silverware immediately.

After a few bites, Josie leaned forward, her blue eyes bright with genuine earnestness on his face. "But, Jack, that was four months ago. Now Grand Springs faces the same issues all the other cities face. Grand Springs got three days of prime-time coverage, then the news moved on. And the people and donations moved with it. People donated enough alfalfa to feed a cow for one day, when we have to get that cow through a year. They helped rebuild a barn, but there is no livestock to fill the stalls. We are just at the beginning of the recovery process and people have already forgotten. Now they've moved on to the next TV show while we have nine months of serious cleanup ahead of us. I'm not sure how we're going to get through it yet. Hal, he just doesn't…''

Her voice broke, her frustration clear. Abruptly, she withdrew, cutting another bit of turkey with rapt attention. ''Well, the next year will be a long one.''

He studied her. ''I bet you have a few ideas on how to get through it.''

''Of course, it's my job. Besides, we're hardly the first community to have to wrestle with this.'' She popped a piece of turkey into her mouth, chewed and swallowed. When she spoke next, she punctuated her words with gesturing silverware. ''There are lots of places to look at, lots of programs that have been tried elsewhere with various degrees of success. My personal favorite is the adopt-a-farm program, which gives the farmer support for a whole year. Or there are livestock donation programs, but that still leaves you with the issue of having to feed new stock when you don't have fields or grain. Well, I've looked into it. I've written enough reports on the subject to fill a damn library. Hopefully, we'll get somewhere soon.''

''But working with Hal is frustrating?''

She shot him a look. ''You ought to know as well as anyone.''

He could hardly refute that. ''Hal's just the acting mayor, you know. We'll have elections for a new mayor soon.''

''Yeah.'' She appeared distracted, attacking the stuffing.

''Ever thought of running?'' Jack asked neutrally.

''Who, me? No way. I don't have the temperament for politics. The first time the school board tenured a bad teacher, I'd feel compelled to tan their hides. And maybe run the teacher out of town on a rail. Hmm, it's a thought. Frankly, I'm still not sure why I'm the treasurer. Olivia can be very persuasive. I mean—'' Her voice faltered. Her gaze dropped to her almost empty plate. "I mean, Olivia could be very persuasive," she finished quietly.

That quickly, the light banked in her face. Her body seemed to curl in on itself. He could sense the grief that ran through her like a river. It shook him. He hadn't seen grief like that since his older brother had died.

"You…you miss her?"

She smiled dryly. "Of course. Olivia was like a mother to me, but you don't want to hear that, do you, Detective? You want me to be the evil town treasurer, plotting some political coup. Do you think I'm so dense I can't see through your questions?"

"I…I…" He didn't know what to say.

She shook her head. "You are so transparent. Cops are nothing more than bureaucrats, you know. You have Hal breathing down your neck, and his marching orders are clear—find who killed Olivia Stuart. From what I've heard, you have no real evidence, no real clues. So what do your little minds do? They manufacture this preposterous scheme where the overworked town treasurer decides to murder her best friend so she can earn forty-five thousand a year as the overworked mayor of a town devastated by mud slides and a growing drug problem. Too bad Olivia didn't have a butler, Jack. Then you could've just arrested him and saved us all some grief."

"That's enough."

His voice was so controlled, it took her a minute to realize that he was angry. Very, very angry. Her stomach did that crazy flip-flop again.

"Why?" she found herself pushing. The blood hummed in her ears. The air picked up between them, and she knew she wasn't the only one who felt it. She challenged him openly, knowing that she shouldn't but unable to resist. "Tell me what I said that wasn't true."

"I am not looking for *convenient* answers, Josie, not even to get Hal Stuart off my back. I'm looking for the right answer. I want to know who killed Olivia Stuart. You had opportunity. You fit the description. You obviously don't like cops—"

"So sue me."

"You keep to yourself and you never talk about your family, where you're from. In my book, you obviously have something to hide."

Her pulse accelerated. She wanted to yell no, she wanted to push away. She was so shaken, she remained sitting right where she was.

"I went to school in upstate New York," she said abruptly. "Both my parents died when I was twelve. I was raised in a foster home. I have no family. I moved to Grand Springs because I wanted roots. I took the job because Olivia Stuart made me believe I could be good at it. She made me believe I'd found a home. Any other questions, Detective?"

She pushed away her plate. Now she could stand. She looked down at him with all the disdain she could muster and threw eight bucks on the table to cover her half of the meal.

"I know my rights. Next time you want to talk to me, it's going to take more than a cheap dinner, Jack Stryker. You'd better show up with a subpoena or don't show up at all. Too bad, too. I'd rather enjoyed talking with you. Well, that'll teach me."

She pivoted neatly in her heels and, with the aplomb of a duchess, walked away.

Jack watched her retreat with frustration, wanting to stop her, not knowing what to say. He just didn't have the answers.

His turkey congealed in the gravy on his plate. He pushed it away with more force than necessary. Damn, damn, damn.

Four

"So what is your sign?"

Josie looked up from the buffet table where she was adjusting the garlands of fresh flowers trimming the punch bowl. Jack Stryker stared down at her, an assessing look in his eye. She'd half expected to hear from him today—certainly his reputation for persistence indicated he wouldn't let her go after one messy dinner. Instead, she'd made it through her workday with only the usual hassles. She'd left work at five to help set up the high school gym for the Band, Bingo, Bake Sale fund-raiser. They'd just gotten the last of the balloons up when people started arriving. Now the lights were dim, the buffet table full, and the gym floor vibrated with gaily dressed couples doing the two-step.

She noticed Jack had exchanged his usual suit for jeans, a western dress shirt, a wide belt and well-worn boots. The shirt was deep blue and accentuated his eyes. The belt, with its tasteful silver buckle, brought her gaze to his trim waist. The heeled boots made his long, lean legs even longer and leaner. Damn him.

Abruptly, she stabbed her finger at the nuclear red punch. "I helped mix that. Wanna test it for poison?"

Then she turned and walked away.

He caught her elbow before she cleared the buffet table and pulled her up short. She shot him through with a single meaningful gaze. "I'm warning you, I'm a murder suspect.

Hanging out with me could ruin your Boy Scout reputation.''

"I'm a cop. I'm supposed to spend time with murder suspects. Would you like to dance?''

"Oh geez, and you asked that so sweetly. But sorry, I'm a city girl. I don't two-step.''

"I'll teach you how.''

"No. No, no, no.''

He'd already swept her into the dance area, his palm firm and warm on the small of her back. He had strong hands. Good feet, too. She stepped on his boots twice just to make him pay for kidnapping her. He didn't appear to notice.

"Work still busy?'' he murmured in her ear as he swung her around.

She was wearing a simple cotton dress of deep purple flowers blooming on white. The flared skirt swirled around her bare legs in a rather heady sensation. Her traitorous blond hair was clipped back in a large barrette. Now she wished she'd left it down so his hands could run through it.

Okay, stop it right now, imagination. I'm warning you...

"Work?'' he prompted again, swinging her around.

"Busy enough,'' she answered belatedly as he pulled her back against his hard torso.

"Aren't you going to ask about my day?''

They moved back. Wait, they moved forward. How did people make this look so simple?

"All right,'' she muttered, her focus on his quick-moving feet. "Did you torture any small animals today, put any innocent people on the rack?''

"Only one or two.''

"Ah, slow day at the office.'' He dipped her abruptly. She found herself staring at the ceiling, then suddenly she was vertical again.

"Well, the thumbscrews are still being fixed. There's not much we can do without them."

"That's understandable." Her voice was getting breathless. "Where's your 'date'?"

"My father's probably at the bake sale. My mother's an excellent cook, but she watches her sugar intake—doctor's advice—and my father has the world's worst sweet tooth. Let out of the house, he's been known to binge. I would imagine right about now he's searching out the biggest, gooeyest pecan pie he can find. By midnight, he'll be tucked in a corner with a fork, shoveling for all he's worth. I'll probably have to drive him home high as a kite and with pecans smeared all over his cheeks."

"Ah, a sugarholic, huh?"

"Of the worst kind. Don't tell anyone. The man has his reputation to consider."

"Ben's secret is safe with me."

The music ended. Somehow Jack was guiding her toward the far end of the gym, where no lights or people intruded. She struggled briefly. He simply walked faster.

"Big brute," she muttered under her breath, tugging to free her arm.

"I just want to talk," he said soothingly.

"Well, I just want to win the lottery. When I get my wish, you can have yours." She finally jerked her arm free, rubbing her elbow though his grip hadn't been bruising. "Just so you know, I don't go for the he-man type."

"That's what I wanted to ask you about." Having succeeded in getting her into the corner, he now planted his hand above her head, pinning her against the wall. He stood much too close. She could smell fresh aftershave and soap. Maybe a hint of toothpaste. His lean cheeks held a faint sheen from dancing. She wanted to wipe the dewdrops from his forehead with her fingertips. Then she wanted to trace the line of his jaw, discover the rasp of his beard.

Dammit, didn't he know cops were supposed to be fat and puffy?

She fidgeted with her cotton dress, hating the traitorous tremor in her hands. Her dress was sedate enough—as town treasurer, she was very conscientious about her appearance. The sheer lace teddy and bra she wore beneath the dress, on the other hand... Lately, her lingerie habit had been way out of control.

Worse, this morning she'd found herself staring at her drawer filled with lingerie, wondering if Jack liked white, black or red. He struck her as a pastel man—pale pink, mint green, baby blue, creamy peach.

Tonight, God help her, she'd selected creamy peach.

She stared at Jack hotly, ready to blame him for all the riotous thoughts, doubts and fears that occupied her mind these days. Her father's daughter, she came out of the gate swinging.

"I already told you, if you want to ask me any questions, you need a subpoena."

"I got that message last night. So today, I asked Rio questions instead. He speaks very highly of you."

"Oh." She was slightly mollified. She liked Rio Redtree a great deal. The *Grand Springs Herald*'s top investigative reporter was as shrewd and brilliant as they came. His report on Hal's stock holdings in one of the strip mining companies had certainly taken the wind out of the acting mayor's sails. Josie was prepared to love the man for that alone. Rio had just married Olivia's daughter, Eve, and they were now a very happy couple with their five-year-old daughter Molly. Grand Springs seemed to be filled with happy couples these days. Josie began scowling again.

"Rio mentioned your involvement in all the rebuilding activities. He seems to think you're God's gift to fund-raising."

"Rio is an excellent judge of character."

"Uh-huh. He was rather surprised by your decision to date Don Matthews. You know, the druggist." His voice went from casual to intent in less than a heartbeat.

"My, my, you have been busy," Josie murmured. She was no longer amused.

"I spoke to Don, too."

"I bet you did."

"He says you two had a 'nice time' together."

Josie snorted with disdain. "Don Matthews is the most egocentric, narcissistic man I've ever had the misfortune of meeting. Present company excluded, of course."

"Thank you. He said you expressed a great deal of interest in his work."

"Of course I expressed a great deal of interest in his work. Frankly, mixing liquids is the only exciting thing about the man. It was either that or spend a whole dinner listening to 'blah-blah *Porsche,* blah-blah *condo,* blah-blah *my cellular phone,* blah-blah *my stockbroker.*' The man obviously got his conversational training from Donald Trump."

"Come on, Josie. The man took you to Randolphs, the most expensive restaurant around. How boring could it have been?"

"Well, let's see. Before we finished the appetizer, I was already making mental notes to pick up my dry cleaning and get my teeth cleaned. That's always an indication of a good time."

"Don seemed smitten with you, and a little disappointed that there wasn't a second date. Did you learn everything you needed to know about prescription drugs the first time around?"

"No, I learned everything I needed to know about boredom. And Don wasn't smitten with me. He doesn't even know me. He just wanted to been seen with a blonde." She pushed against Jack's chest. He didn't move. "Jack

Stryker, step back or I'll scream. I'll do it, too, and we both know it.''

''One more question.''

''I don't like your questions!'' She jabbed his chest with her index finger. ''Let me question you, Mr. Hotshot Cop. Did Don say that I asked about pure potassium?''

''No.''

''Did he report that I got any prescriptions or medication from him?''

''Did you?''

''No, I did not, you most insufferable man! And I would hope he didn't tell you otherwise.''

''He didn't tell me otherwise.''

''Then, why are we having this conversation? What crime did I commit—other than a violation of common sense—by going on a date with Don Matthews?''

''Why did you go out with him, Josie?''

She stared at him a moment, then abruptly she shook her head. ''You just don't get it, do you, Stryker? I went out with Don because he *asked*. He didn't appear to have a contagious disease or a hidden wedding band, so what the hell, I decided to spend one night doing something other than watching the late show. Lord have mercy on my soul.''

He was quiet, his hand still above her head. Her diatribe had left her exhausted. She just stood there, feeling his gaze upon her cheeks. It lowered slowly. She closed her eyes and felt his look caressing her throat.

''Why don't you make this easy on us both,'' he whispered. ''Why don't you just tell me what it is you're hiding.''

''I'm not hiding anything.''

''Now you're lying.''

''You have an overactive imagination. I'm just an accountant, Jack, not the missing link. I work too hard. I go home late at night to a house with dying plants and dust so thick that a single sneeze starts sandstorms in three rooms. It's a glamorous life, but someone's got to lead it.''

"Tell me about your parents.''

Her eyes opened. She shook her head.

"Why not?''

"Because it hurts, Jack. Because it's no one's business but mine. Just like your brother Tom's death is no one's business but yours.''

He flinched, then quickly lowered his head. "Ben,'' he said at last, his gaze on the floor. "Ben told you.''

"He mentioned it, yes. He said he'd had a son Tom. But Tom had had a motorcycle. And Tom had liked to drink beer.''

"It was such a stupid thing to do,'' Jack muttered. He still wouldn't look at her. She wished he would. She could hear the emotion in the thickness of his voice.

"How old was he?''

"Eighteen.''

"How old were you?''

"Fourteen.''

"Just old enough to idolize him.''

"He was something. Grand Springs's rebel without a clue.'' Jack abruptly cleared his throat. His eyes narrowed and she could see him pulling himself together. "I'm not here to talk about Tom.''

"No, you're here at a social fund-raiser interrogating the woman who helped put it together. Straight Arrow Stryker, always on the job. Well, that's impressive. I hope you sleep well at night. As for me, I can see that the punch is running low. Goodbye.''

She pushed in earnest this time, catching him off guard and managing to break free. He didn't try to stop her. She suppressed the tiny desire for him to do so and kept walking.

In front of her, the band played loudly and people stomped to the beat. Strobe lights flickered across the gymnasium floor and laughing dancers. From the outskirts, Josie watched a young couple scoot into a quick embrace. She was unbearably aware of the feel of her lace teddy against her skin and Jack's gaze on her back.

Dammit, there was so much more to life than what she had, but she didn't know how to find it. Her breathing was still uneven from speaking to Jack, but for him it had been only business. Why couldn't he see beyond his own suspicions? Why couldn't he let his work ethic go for just one moment and dance with her because he wanted her in his arms, not because he was thinking of her behind bars?

And why was she so foolish as to want such things with him? And how could she be so traitorous as to admire his work ethic and be impressed by his sense of duty?

She stood amid laughing, stomping people, Jack's gaze still on her.

She refused to turn around.

For the rest of the evening, Jack roamed the gymnasium restlessly. It occurred to him that over the last four months, a lot of things in Grand Springs had changed and he'd been working too hard to consider any of them. Generally, he hung out with Stone at social functions. But Stone was now married and out on the dance floor with Jessie. Jack had also spent a lot of time with Rio. Now Rio played bingo with his Eve and their daughter Molly.

Jack walked alone and his gaze kept returning to Josie. She was easy to spot. The strobe lighting made the white backdrop of her dress glow, until she moved around the dim outskirts of the gym like a firefly. She mingled effortlessly, constantly greeting and exchanging pleasantries with most of the people present. She seemed to know everyone, and yet none of the conversations were long. She said hello, exchanged a few laughs and moved on.

She gave him a wide berth. Stone, as well. In fact, of the six police officers present, he never saw her say hi to any of them. Once, when he finally had a chance to talk to Stone and Jessie, he thought he felt someone watching him and pivoted just in time to catch her turning away.

He couldn't keep from seeking her with his gaze again. He wanted to talk to her. He couldn't think of anything more to say. He hadn't felt this nervous and wound up since he'd walked past a downtown beauty parlor and seen Marjorie working in the window. It had taken him two weeks to work up the courage to ask her out.

Six months later, he'd rubbed his sweating palms against his pant legs as he prepared to ask her to be his wife. She'd looked so beautiful that night. Dark hair cascading down to her waist, sultry eyes, heavy-lidded and twinkling with a secret smile...

Jack shook the thoughts away. He didn't want to re- member Marjorie or the life he'd thought they would have together, because then he'd have to remember her flashing brown limbs as she scrambled out of their bed and young Officer Horrock's embrace.

He'd have to remember standing in the doorway, his face expressionless and his gut cold as he realized that it was over. His marriage had failed. He had failed.

By eleven o'clock, Jack had had enough of the fund-raiser. He was tired. His shoulders were tight. He was wor-ried about the Olivia Stuart case, plus he had a lot of work to do on the other eight files sitting on his desk. He was thinking he would go into work first thing tomorrow morn-ing, then he was thinking maybe he'd go in tonight.

It seemed easier to go to work than to lie in his shad-owed bedroom, staring at the ceiling at 4:00 a.m. and wor-rying about all the things he needed to get done. Josie had been right last night. The rebuilding of Grand Springs was just beginning. And Jack felt the enormous pressure of the work ahead.

He sought out his father, finding him by the bake sale area. Sure enough, Ben was polishing off a pecan pie.

"Ready to go?"

"I feel sick."

"You just ate a whole pecan pie, Dad."

"Yeah. And boy was it good." Ben's smile was completely without regret. Jack shook his head while his father scrubbed his sticky cheeks with a napkin.

They headed across the gym together, Jack still trying to pick out Josie. For a change, she was nowhere to be seen. His restlessness grew. It bothered him to leave without at least seeing her again.

What would you say to her, Jack? What would you say?

"I saw her leave," his father commented.

"Who?"

"The person you're not looking for," his father said sagely.

Jack drove with his jaw tight and the muscles knotted in his back.

"Nice night," his father remarked at last.

"Yeah, it is."

"Did you enjoy the dance?"

"It was fine."

"Nice girl, Josie. I thought you told your mother you weren't interested in her? From the way I saw you leaning over her in the corner, I'd say you were kinda interested."

"I was just asking her some questions."

"Uh-huh."

They drifted back into silence. There weren't many cars on the road. The night whizzed by, inky black.

"You okay?" Ben asked at last.

"Just got a lot on my mind."

"Work?"

"Yes."

"The Olivia Stuart case?"

"Yes."

Ben looked out the window. "Your mother's worried about you."

"Mom's always worried about me."

"Yes, but for a change, I agree with her."

Jack was honestly startled. He looked over at his father. "I'm fine, Dad. Really. I just have a lot of work to do. Crime rate's up, we're short-staffed, and we have a couple of major cases on our plate. Plus, we've got a temporary mayor. Things'll slow back down eventually."

"You were always very intense, Jack."

Jack shrugged. He felt cornered and he didn't know why. He and his father rarely had conversations like this.

"You were a very intent little boy," his father continued after a moment. "Tom was a happy child, always laughing and getting into trouble. You were serious from the day you were born. I still remember you sitting on the carpet, couldn't have been more than one or two, picking out all the debris and arranging it in perfect geometric patterns. Your mom was so embarrassed she started vacuuming every two days."

"I'm just a little overworked, Dad. That's all."

"Then Tom started getting into trouble, staying out late, building the motorcycle. There was just something wild in that boy. I never did get it. He reminded me a bit of my older brother. Maybe that was it. Tom got into trouble. You got more serious."

Jack fell silent. He didn't know what to say.

"I remember the night the call came," Ben said abruptly. "I remember having to tell your mom that Tom was dead. She cried so hard her whole body shook. I couldn't get her to stop shaking. You walked into the living room then. It was two in the morning."

"Yes."

"I told you that Tom had been in an accident. That Tom was dead. Do you know what you said?"

"No," Jack whispered.

"You looked over at your mother, who was still crying, and you said, 'Will she be all right?' I said, 'In a bit.' You nodded and went back to bed. I never saw you cry, Jack. Even at the funeral, you stood there like a solider, holding your mother's hand while she wailed and wailed and wailed. I had to take her to the hospital soon after that.''

Jack nodded. He remembered what had happened next. His mother had been in the hospital for six months. It had been just him and his father in the house, and the pall of the son and brother that was no more. They had moved in silence. That's all Jack really recalled from that period of time. The eerie silence.

Then his mother had returned and the silence became a persistent undercurrent. The need to not talk too loud, not walk too loud, not be too loud. Sometimes he would wake up in the middle of the night and his mother would be standing in his room, watching him sleep as if she needed to reassure herself that he, at least, was still there. Once, when he was ten minutes late coming home from football practice, he found her collapsed in the living room, crying so hard she hiccuped uncontrollably. How could he put her through that? she yelled hysterically when he brushed her shoulder. How could he scare her like that?

He was very careful never to be late again. He became very careful of a lot of things, moving through life as if he were wading through cotton, each movement slow and deliberate so he wouldn't disturb his mother and her fragile nerves. It had felt like that ever since.

"Do you still love her?" he asked his father quietly. He'd never asked before, but this seemed to be the night for it.

"Yes," his father said without hesitation. "Of course I love your mother. I remember the girl she was, how she would toss her hair over her shoulder when she sipped her cherry Coke. That used to drive me wild. I remember the look on her face when she held out each of you kids to me in the hospital, her face all shiny with sweat, her expression bursting with pride. She was quite a woman, Jack.

She still is. You have a lot of your mother in you, you know?''

Jack automatically shook his head. Ben abruptly twisted in the passenger's seat to face him.

''I'm muddling this,'' his father said. ''But in my own way, this is what I'm trying to tell you—you're too intense. You bottle things up too much. Look at yourself these days, Jack. You've got shadows under your eyes. You've lost weight. You don't smile anymore. When was the last time you went out? When was the last time you let yourself go a little?

''You try too hard to control everything, to be too perfect. You're like your mother that way, you both want everything to go just so. It doesn't work, Jack. Life is messy. Floods wipe out farms. Children turn eighteen, drink beer and get killed on motorcycles.'' His voice gentled. ''And beautiful first wives turn out to be lying, conniving women who cheat on their husbands.''

Jack's hands tightened on the wheel. ''I don't understand—''

''Of course you don't.'' Ben turned back to the window, his mood still expansive. ''I hit you out of the blue with all this, I know that. I was just sitting there tonight, eating my pecan pie, watching the people dance, and I thought, I'm a happy man. I love my wife. I love my son. I love my town. I am happy, Jack. That's what nights like tonight are all about. That life is messy, but it's okay because we can all clean up together. I don't think you and your mother get that. You think you have to keep everything just in place. Then when it falls and breaks, you think only you can put it back together again. And when you can't, you shoulder the failure like a permanent burden. Your mom eats staring at an empty chair. You work yourself into the ground, not even able to say her name. This family has too many ghosts.''

''All that sugar's gone to your head, Dad.''

"Maybe. Maybe not. Next time, I'll make you eat a pie, too."

Jack flexed his fingers on the car wheel. They were nearing his parents' house. He began to slow.

"Relax a little," Ben said softly. "Sleep a little. Put back on some weight. And for God's sake, ask Josie Reynolds out on a date. She's nothing like Marjorie—your mom was right about her. Now, Josie, I know. Josie's a good girl."

Jack just nodded as he pulled into the driveway and his father opened the door. He didn't know how to tell his exuberant father that Josie might be beautiful, and Josie might be sweet, but she was also the number one suspect in a murder investigation.

He waited until his father had gone into the house, then he pulled out again.

The night was still silent, thick. Suddenly, it stifled him. He drove, but he was no longer heading toward his one-bedroom bachelor pad with the brown carpet he'd never liked and the stiff, Spartan furniture that had never been comfortable. He'd never liked being a bachelor, not in his teens and not in his thirties. When he came home at night and looked around him, he just saw too much silence again.

He wanted noise. He wanted to build a family to be how his family had once been—rowdy, laughing and fighting. He missed the days when Tom had been alive. The boisterousness. The raw, uninhibited energy.

The honesty.

He found himself pulling into a small suburban enclave of Grand Springs. At this time of night, most of the houses were dark, just porch lights illuminating the way for wayward children or spouses to return home.

The driveway he pulled into didn't have any lights visible at all. The small house was completely still, completely dark.

He sat in the driveway one last moment, thinking he should just drive away. Go home. Go to work.

He got out of the car.

And knocked on the door of Josie's place.

Five

"What are you doing here?" Josie answered his second knock. Her blond hair was still clipped back at the nape of her neck, but she was now wearing a red silk kimono bathrobe and her face was dewy soft, as if it had just been scrubbed. Damp tendrils of hair curled around her temples.

He stared at her, the delicate arch of her pale eyebrows, the slant of her porcelain blue eyes. The light flush of color slowly seeping up her cheeks from her neck.

"Stryker?"

His gaze settled on her lips. They parted abruptly. "This is *not* a good idea," she said.

"I agree." He walked into her house. The lights were off in the living room, but a pale glow down the hall indicated where her bedroom must be. He veered away sharply, pacing a small circle and waiting for common sense to slap him back to reality.

Stryker, what are you doing? His hands were trembling.

Josie stood in front of the closed door, her eyes locked on his face.

"You still think I'm a suspect, don't you, Jack?"

"Yes." He took a step toward her.

"You're still wondering if you can trust me."

"Yes." He took another step.

"You're not even sure if you like me."

"Yes." He trapped her against the closed door. "But I want you, Josie."

Her breath left her in a rush. Her jaw worked several

times, but no words came out. Her gaze was transfixed on his face, then slowly, it settled onto his lips.

"I know I shouldn't," he whispered. "I know. Only I think I'm going to do it, anyway." He planted his hands on either side of her head. He searched her gaze with his. Then slowly, he reached back, found the barrette holding her hair and unclipped it. The silky strands slid forward with a sigh, like water finally overflowing a dam. Even in the darkness, her hair glowed like spun gold.

"Smells like apples and strawberries," he murmured, picking up a fistful, then letting it drop.

"Shampoo," Josie muttered weakly. Her eyes had gone pleading. "You don't really want to do this, Jack. I know your type. Military haircuts, razor-pressed suits. I don't even make my bed in the morning."

"I figured as much." He ran his fingertips down her cheek, catching a last drop of water and rolling it between his forefinger and thumb. He was fascinated by the feel of the water, the softness of her skin.

"Look around. I haven't cleaned this place in months. Dead plants, dishes in the sink, dust over everything, I swear to God. And laundry? Don't even ask about laundry. If it wasn't for my very patient dry cleaner who can turn around a blouse in an hour, I wouldn't be fit to show up in an office."

"I iron my shirts every morning," he confessed. His hand slipped to the edge of her silk robe. "With spray starch."

"Oh God," she moaned. "Spray starch. I'm not even sure what that is!"

"What are you wearing beneath this robe, Josie? It's been driving me crazy, those little glimpses of lace beneath your prim-and-proper suits. How did an accountant end up with so much lingerie?"

"Stupidity!" she exclaimed desperately. "Sheer, unadulterated stupidity! Oh, God, Jack, go away before you kill us both!''

He couldn't. He should, but he couldn't. He was watching her breasts tighten beneath their thin cover of red silk. He was thinking he'd never wanted anything like he wanted to touch her right now. His carefully controlled life seemed to have boiled down to this one moment when his hand enfolded the soft curve of her breast and her breath escaped as a sigh.

He brushed her lips with his for the first time. She tasted the way he thought she would—not sweet, but hot. Real. Honest. Vital. There was nothing weak or fragile about Josie Reynolds. And nothing conniving or shallow. ''Tell me you want me.''

''No, I don't. I could never possibly want a cop!''

He caught her lower lip. He pulled it into his mouth and sucked lavishly. Her neck arched, her hands unfurled on his shoulders. He angled his head and kissed her deeply, wet, hot and hungry. With a moan, she clamped her arms around his neck. Her body pressed against him, her lips welcoming. His tongue tangled with hers and she gave as good as she got, her fingers digging into his scalp and pulling him closer.

He broke away abruptly, his breath ragged, his eyes glittery.

''You want me,'' he stated roughly.

''Maybe the teeniest, tiniest bit,'' she admitted hoarsely, and dragged his head back down.

It was an eating kiss. He sucked on her lips, she chewed on his chin. Somehow he had her pressed up hard against the door, and her hands were tugging at his shirt as if she'd shred every fiber. He found the knotted belt around her waist and yanked it free. The kid who'd waited very patiently every Christmas morning to open his presents turned into the man who ripped silk from her lithe frame.

He discovered sheer peach lace and shimmering peach satin. "Oh, my."

"You like peach?"

"Honey, you could be wearing desert camo and I'd be happy." His hands roamed down her torso, exploring the lean feel of her rib cage, the soft indent of her waist, the generous curve of her hips. He didn't know where to begin anymore.

"I haven't done this in a while," she whispered.

"Me, neither." He scooped her up in his arms and headed toward the beckoning bedroom light. He didn't want to think. For just one moment, Straight Arrow Stryker wanted to follow the thrum of adrenaline in his ears.

He tossed her onto the middle of a feather mattress, then clawed his way through the piles of soft, brilliant pillows to find her. Her hands were tugging on his shirt again, grabbing the edge and pulling so hard it went, snap, snap, snap, all the way down. Her mouth closed over the smooth expanse of his bare collarbone. Her tongue tasted him. He went a little nuts.

Together, they tossed all the pillows aside; plumes of goose down and swathes of floral sheets billowed up. Next, they attacked his clothes like two greedy children, strewing shoes, socks, belt, jeans and underwear all over the floor.

"You have no hair on your chest." She sighed.

"That okay?"

"That's perfect." Her hands drifted lower, finding his naked flanks. "Oh. Oh, goodness." She sighed with open appreciation and squeezed hard enough to give him goose bumps.

"You're wearing too many clothes," he informed her thickly.

"Get them off, get them off!"

He had to take a deep breath before he could handle the teddy. His fingers seemed to be shaking abnormally hard, and he didn't want to tear the fragile material. When his fingers moved between her legs to find the snaps, she was already so hot and wet he forgot his purpose and stroked her instead. She fell back against the soft feather mattress, her hair pooled around her, her eyes heavy-lidded. The bedside lamp was on, but she didn't turn it off.

She looked at him with frank longing, and it was the most beautiful, intoxicating sight he'd ever seen. When he finally unsnapped the teddy and pulled the fabric up, she whimpered at the loss of his touch. Her hands settled on his belly. Then they folded around him and squeezed gently.

He almost took her right then.

"Protection?" he whispered hoarsely.

She looked up at him blankly, her hands still moving, her hips still writhing. He closed his eyes and forced his lips to move through the languorous fog building in his mind. "Josie, are you on the pill?"

"The...the pill?" Abruptly, her hands fell away. His eyes opened. She was sitting straight up and her face was stricken.

"I'm not on the pill," she confessed in a rush. "I don't do things like sleep with men I hardly know and who think I may have killed my best friend. Other than that, do you have condoms?"

"Uh-oh."

"Ah!" She hit his shoulder. "I thought you were a Boy Scout! What happened to Be Prepared?"

"I don't know!" he yelled right back. "I don't generally sleep with women I hardly know who hate me just because I wear a badge. Other than that...wanna do some heavy petting?"

"Okay."

He fell on top of her, kissing her deeply. The touch of her skin against him was electric, the feel of her fingernails against his back, divine. "This is a bad idea," he whispered over and over again, then devoured her mouth.

"Shut up and put your hand right…there. Oh, yes, right there."

He cupped her breast and she melted beneath him. He lowered his head and drew the hard bead of her nipple into her mouth. He sucked hard and squeezed his eyes against the bolts of desire driving up to his groin.

"Stryker…" Her fingers curled into his hair, massaging his scalp, telling him what he was doing to her. He laved her nipple generously, then nibbled tiny love bites down to the indent of her waist. He tongued her belly button.

"Oh my, oh my, oh my," she moaned. He stuck his finger in her mouth to shut her up. She sucked on the offered digit suggestively enough to seduce a saint.

He spread her legs and found her with his mouth.

Her first scream of release caught him off guard. He clutched her convulsing hips with his hands, pinning her in place as he devoured her more thoroughly. Her hands dug into his shoulders. She whimpered, moaned his name and thrashed her head to the side.

The roar built in his ears. He could hear his own heart beating in his veins. She convulsed the second time, and the power of it ripped through him. He wanted… He needed…

God, he hadn't known anything about anything until he'd held this woman and tasted her skin.

She drew him up desperately. He was too far gone to think anymore.

"Let me, let me," she whispered. He let her. Her fingers found him, tightened and stroked, and he toppled over the edge with his teeth clamping his lower lip. He was falling, down, down, down. Her mouth was on his shoulder. He could taste the salt from her skin.

He buried his face against her hair, inhaled the scent of

strawberries one last time, and for the first time in months, life felt all right.

Everything was going to be all right.

He cradled her against his shuddering body and their breathing finally eased. They both drifted into sleep.

"Hey, you are not even trying!"

"I am, too," he protested. "Okay, okay, one more time. I swear I'll get it."

He opened his mouth wide, she obediently tossed the kernel of popcorn high into the air. He bobbed too soon and the kernel bounced off his nose. She shook her head.

"Stryker, Stryker, Stryker, how have you made it through life?"

It was 7:00 a.m. on Saturday morning. Generally, she was waking up right about now and contemplating dragging her lazy butt to work. Instead, she was sprawled on her bed in her red silk kimono, bearing a large bowl of microwave popcorn—the only food she had in the house. Jack was leaning against a plush stack of pillows, clad only in his white B.V.D.s—he'd struck her as a B.V.D. man from the very beginning. On the other hand, she imagined it had taken him until last night to figure out her secret lingerie fetish. The knowledge made her smug.

She popped another kernel into the air and caught it effortlessly between her teeth, chomping noisily. "Really, Stryker, what did you do growing up, anyway?"

"Hiking, camping, hunting, fishing," he said promptly. "I can name most birds and identify most trees. Oh, I also know how to tie a dozen different kinds of knots." He waggled a brow, devilishly handsome in just his underwear. "Want me to prove it?"

She grinned, ridiculously pleased by the fun side of Jack Stryker. She never would have guessed a stuffed shirt like him had quite so many...nuances. And she couldn't remember when she'd last felt so relaxed. She wasn't sure she wanted to dwell on it.

She tossed another kernel into the air. At least it hit his lip this time. He recovered it with his fingers and stuffed it in the old-fashioned way. He settled more deeply into the pile of pillows, picked up a strand of her hair and wrapped it around his finger.

"I think this bed is the most decadent thing I've ever experienced," he said.

"Honey, that wasn't the bed."

"Oh." For a moment, he appeared close to blushing. That made her grin more. He shook his head. "And you dress like such a sweet, young thing."

"I'm a treasurer. Appearances are important."

"People speak very highly of you, Josie. They say you look like an angel and work like a dog."

"They do?" That made her genuinely happy. Someone like Jack had had credibility and trust since his first waking moment. Things had worked a little differently for Josie. The life she'd built in Grand Springs, the job she took so seriously, were valued by her precisely because of how hard she'd had to work to get them. And in a perfect world, she'd be the only person who would ever know exactly how far she'd come.

Jack's gaze had grown sober and contemplative. She threw more popcorn into the air, not willing to let it end so soon.

"So how long had it been, Stryker?"

"How long what?"

"Since you had sex. You said it had been a while."

She had the pleasure of seeing his eyes widen, then blink. Jack Stryker was officially flummoxed. "I wasn't the first person since Marjorie, was I?" Josie asked in sudden shock. "A man who looks like you, I would imagine you get plenty of offers."

"Well... I mean..." He was definitely blushing. He shook his head, chagrined. "There were a few women afterward. You know—the 'get back on the horse' sorta thing. But nothing...serious. It's...uh, it's been a few years. And we haven't exactly had sex yet, for the record."

She shrugged. "Close enough." She volunteered on her own, "Four years."

"*Four years?* To quote someone I know, 'A woman who looks like you, I would imagine you get plenty of offers.'"

"Oh, sure, but most of the men doing the offering could be pinups in a Creep-of-the-Month calendar. The truth is, Stryker, that good men are an endangered species in most towns. My theory is that it's due to women's natural superiority over men—"

"Do I really want to hear this?"

"Absolutely. See, when a woman finds a good man, she doesn't doubt it. She recognizes gold when she sees it and she takes him out of circulation. A man, on the other hand, will encounter a perfectly good woman, hem and haw over whether or not there might be some elusive better woman somewhere out there, and walk away. Thus, good women are a dime a dozen, and good men are nowhere to be found."

"I see."

"Stryker, stay a bit, will you?"

He studied her a moment longer. His fingers brushed her lips. "All right," he said quietly. "I will."

"These are your parents?" He held up the silver-framed portrait from the bedside table. It was 10:00 a.m. now, morning was fully upon them, and reality seeped in as surely as the rays of sun snaking through the venetian blinds. Josie lay against him, her head on his shoulder, her hair mussed, her body covered only by shifting swathes of red silk. He'd been holding her for hours and his body was hard again. He didn't do anything about it. They still didn't have any protection, and he didn't think it would be right to seduce her once more, then simply walk out the door. Besides, it had been a long time since he'd lain with a lithe body curled up next to his, hair tickling his nose, weight putting his arm to sleep. She felt good. Better than he would've thought. Better than he was prepared for.

What had his father told him? *Life is messy.*

He returned his focus to the portrait. It was old, the color having faded to a yellowish-green tone, the way old film was prone to do. The smiles on everyone's faces, however, were still brilliant. The man was big and heavy, his sandy blond hair cut a little wild and his suit ill-fitting. He looked at the camera frankly, however, and the laughter and love in his eyes were unmistakable. He had his arms around a petite, ethereal blonde in a simple pink dress and a bit more wisdom in her eyes. She leaned into the man's embrace, not just accepting it, but returning it as if it were the most natural thing in the world. The two simply fit. Before them sat a little girl in cutoff shorts, a too-big T-shirt and a gap-toothed smile. Her hair had been hastily clipped back, but blond strands still curled riotously around her cheeks and temples. Her smile, the tilt of her chin and the twinkle in her eye marked her as Josie.

"They look very much in love," he said at last. Josie had stiffened beside him, but she hadn't pulled away. Her finger doodled a small, unconscious circle on his shoulder while her gaze remained locked on the portrait.

"Her name was Rose," she said softly, and pointed at her mother. "And that's Stan. They were perfect for each other."

"Was it an accident?" He felt her resistance in the subtle changes of her body. The inch of air that appeared as she shifted slightly away, the loss of warmth as she curled more tightly in on herself.

"Something like that." A vague answer. The man in him was hurt, the cop in him suspicious. He carefully returned the portrait to the bedside table.

"The hardest part, I find," he said finally, "is the need to remember the people you've lost. The burden of it. Because if you don't remember them...if you don't tell the stories of your brother's sixth birthday or the day he learned how to drive or the time he taught you to fish, then no one will know who he was. He really will be gone."

Josie turned in his embrace. She looked at him, something vulnerable and tentative in her eyes. "I don't have any other relatives," she said abruptly. "No grandparents, no aunts, no uncles. There is no one alive who knew them but me. I'm the only one who remembers just how in love they were, how hard they worked to build some semblance of a home when my father...he really wasn't qualified for much. He did mostly odd jobs—sales—so money came and went. They had their arguments...my mother used to beg him to settle down, but my father was a dreamer. He always had some scheme...." She shrugged. "Then there were the afternoons the three of us would sit in the kitchen eating cookies, and I would think I was the luckiest girl in the world because none of my friends spent their afternoons eating cookies with their parents. No one saw the kind of love I did. And sometimes... Sometimes..."

"Sometimes you're so angry because you loved them so much and they went and died."

"Yes," she said. "Exactly."

"I used to worship Tom," Jack whispered. "I never told my parents that. But when I was little, it just seemed there was nothing he couldn't do. He was wild, he was reckless. He was...he was *beautiful* in his own way. Just to watch him on the football field—no one played the way he played, all fierce and passionate. Afterward he'd rumple my hair because he knew I hated that, and he'd say, 'Don't bother, Jack. Football's too dirty for you.' I'd take a couple of swipes at him, but it made me idolize him even more. Then one night, he drank a six-pack and climbed onto his motorcycle without a helmet.

"What a stupid, stupid thing to do," he blurted out harshly. "For one moment of glory, he killed himself. And he destroyed our mother. She goes through her days now looking at the empty spaces he left. She eats dinner every night staring at his empty chair. Sometimes I hate him for that."

"But you can't hate him," Josie filled in, "because you also love him. And I bet when you finally played your first football game, you wanted to cry afterward because you couldn't tell him about it and prove that you'd finally gotten dirty." Jack was nodding. Her voice picked up. "I went to my prom when I was sixteen. I got all dressed up, and my foster parents, Mr. and Mrs. Brattle, took pictures of me and my date. They were very kind, very supportive, and that made it even worse because I stood there the whole time wanting my mother. I wanted her to be the one to do my hair. I wanted her to help me pick out my dress. I wanted to come home afterward and tell her about dancing and my first kiss. And I couldn't. When I got home, I got so angry I took scissors and cut my dress into little pieces. And then I felt so guilty, I cried."

"I stole one of Tom's football trophies from his room and smashed it in half. Then I spent four nights putting it back together with superglue and tweezers."

"You shattered a trophy?"

"Even Boy Scouts have tempers."

She nodded slowly, her gaze contemplative. "I'm really glad you came over," she said abruptly. Her chin was up, daring him to deny her words.

"I'm glad I came over, too."

"Why did you, Jack? What am I, your midlife crisis?"

"I don't think being attracted to a beautiful, intelligent accountant really qualifies as a midlife crisis."

"Oh." She blinked her eyes a few times, then abruptly tucked her head against his shoulder. He stroked her hair, unreasonably touched by the small display of shyness. She was something. Blunt, yet mysterious. Bold, yet shy. Serious, but a changeling.

He didn't want to leave, but he couldn't keep his eyes off the clock. It was almost eleven o'clock. He couldn't hide from reality, or his job, forever.

"You have to go," Josie whispered.

"Yes. I do."

She drew away, not meeting his gaze. "Would you like to shower first?"

"Uh…no. I'll, uh, shower back at my place."

"All right. More popcorn?"

"No, I'm fine." He sat up in bed, surveying the floor for his clothes. Pillows were strewn everywhere, the yellow, blue and rose colored comforter dumped haphazardly in a corner. He'd never seen anything quite like it. It took him a minute to find his jeans. He pulled them on with his back to her.

"Are you going to work today?" she asked at last.

"Yes. You?"

"Yes. Always lots of work to be done." Out of the corner of his eye, he saw her drag her hand through her long, tangled hair. She stood, belting the robe more tightly around her middle and looking like she didn't know what to do with herself.

"I'm not very good at this," he said at last, hunting down his shirt.

"Me, neither."

"Even when I was a twenty-something bachelor, I wasn't good at the morning after."

"I don't have much experience," Josie said. Her arms were wrapped around her middle in an unconsciously vulnerable stance.

He snapped up his shirt, struggling for a way to fill the void and not coming up with anything. Quietly, Jack tucked his shirt into his jeans, then recovered his belt.

Josie watched him, also feeling uneasy. The moment was done. She kept searching for something sassy and smart to say, something to ease this knot in her throat. She couldn't think of anything. Now she remembered why she avoided things like jumping into bed with overly attractive men. Afterward, she stood like she was standing here now, feeling empty and hollow and alone. Her house would seem quieter after this, her bed too big. She would lie in the middle trying to catch his scent on her pillows and hating herself for wanting so much.

For missing that brief moment of feeling happy, loved and safe once more.

She busied herself closing her bedroom window. She'd cracked it open last night when she returned from the fundraiser. Her imagination had probably run away from her, but she kept catching the scent of gardenias. Since the night she'd discovered Olivia's body, she hadn't been able to stand that smell.

Stryker pulled on his boots, then stood. "I need to get going."

"Okay." She held the edge of her robe together at her throat. She was having a hard time meeting his eyes.

"I'll call you this afternoon."

"Will you?" Her voice was sharper than she intended.

He took a deep breath, walked over and placed his hands on her shoulders. "I won't lie to you, Josie. My father was telling me just last night that life was supposed to be messy. Well, here we are. This is going to be messy.''

"No kidding.''

"I take my job seriously, you know that. It's one of the things we have in common.''

She stared at him mutinously, making him spell it out. So he did.

"I still have to investigate you, Josie. I have a case to solve and I have to look at all the suspects, regardless of what my personal feelings might be. You'll probably get to see me again in a professional capacity. I'll probably rile that temper of yours. It's my job. I'm going to do it.''

"I didn't kill Olivia, you idiot. She was like a second mother to me.''

His hands fell away. For a moment, he looked genuinely haggard and torn. "I have to do my job, Josie. Can you understand that?''

She scowled. "You're right, you're going to rile my temper.''

"I would...I would like to call you this afternoon. Would that be okay, Josie?''

She didn't answer right away. She wanted to see him again, but she was hurt that he couldn't just accept her statement of innocence. She understood how seriously he took his job, but she wanted him to believe in her, anyway. "Do you trust anyone, Stryker?''

He looked uncomfortable. "I trust my parents.''

"But not anyone female, is that it? Not anyone who might remind you of Marjorie?''

"God, Josie, you are blunt.''

"I just want to know where I stand. It's a fair question.''

He dragged his hand through his hair. "I'm not that good at trusting,'' he admitted at last.

"Because if Marjorie lied to you, then all women must lie?''

"No," he said tightly. "Because I was willing to believe her lies, so I must not have the best judgment. If you must know, she messed around on me, Josie. A lot. I married her thinking she was a sweet, beautiful woman with a big heart. Nope. She was a vain, shallow creature who wanted to be the next mayor's wife, and when she discovered I had no such ambitions, she retaliated by sleeping with anyone who drove a better car or lived in a bigger house. And I had to walk in on her with another man to figure it out. Says great things about my cool, analytical mind, doesn't it?"

Josie blinked her eyes. She couldn't think of a response. Jack no longer looked relaxed or rumpled. Lines squeezed his eyes, his hand was compulsively rubbing the back of his neck. She could feel his tightly reined anger and old hurt from across the small space. Abruptly, he let out a long breath.

"I want to see you again, all right? I was thinking I could take you out to dinner. Maybe we could give this a try, one step at a time. That's all I have to offer, Josie, one step at a time. What do you think about that?"

"I could…I could do one step at a time."

"I was thinking I would go by a drugstore this afternoon."

"Oh." Her eyes got wide. That fast, she felt breathless and quivery. "That…that would be very nice."

"You're sure?"

She nodded her head more vigorously than common decency would dictate, but she was rewarded by Jack's slow, growing smile. His shoulders came down. The lines eased around his eyes.

"I had a really nice night," he said softly.

His tone made her brave enough to approach. She slid her arms around his shoulders, settling her body against him. "I want you," she whispered, "a lot."

His hands spanned her waist, massaging little circles through her thin robe. "A lot, huh?" He brushed her lips once, then twice. "Maybe once I get the 'proper equipment' I can do something about that. Maybe I can make that a lot."

"Promises, promises." She kissed him, longer and deeper than she intended. Her arms tightened around his neck for a moment, and she felt something move within her, something dark and shuddery. Old fear, maybe. New pain.

She liked his arms around her, she liked his forthright approach. But she wondered if even the wild side of Jack Stryker could ever really understand or accept the whole truth about Josie Reynolds.

She stepped back, her gaze carefully averted.

"One step at a time," she murmured.

"One step at a time."

She walked him to the door. They parted with another kiss, slightly more self-conscious. She leaned against her door, watching him get into his car and drive away. It amazed her, the sadness that welled up inside her. It was the other aftereffect of losing people close to you. No goodbye was small. All partings carried an undertone of permanency that tore at her.

Once she'd told her mother she was off to school and had never seen her mother alive again. Once she'd told Olivia she would see her at the wedding and had never seen Olivia alive again.

Once she'd sat across from her broken father in the prison's visiting room, telling him how much she missed him, begging him to fight his sentence so they could be together once more.

And she'd never seen him alive again.

Josie padded into her living room. She should shower, get dressed, go to the office. She turned on the TV, search-

ing out Bugs Bunny because that's what she'd always
watched with Stan.

Then she curled up in the chair, wrapped her arms
around her legs and cradled her forehead against her knees,
letting the bright colors and synthetic laughter pour over
her.

I remember you, Dad. I remember.

Six

At twelve-thirty, Josie finally arrived at her office, freshly showered and garbed in a sensible pair of jeans and a soft lavender plaid shirt. Her hair was down, getting in her face but a welcome relief after five consecutive days of wearing it clipped back. There were few advantages to working on the weekends, but one was the considerably more casual dress code. Of course, the sun was shining when she got out of her car, as Grand Springs was seized by a cool, crisp, perfectly beautiful fall day.

She shook her head. "Working on a beautiful, sunny afternoon. You're a smart girl, Josie. A real Einstein."

Her footsteps rang sharply in the hollow corridor. No other office lights were on—most public servants understood that being paid to work only thirty-six and a half hours a week, meant working only thirty-six-and-a-half-hour weeks. Olivia always told Josie she took her job too seriously. Of course, Olivia had known Josie's hours because she'd been in the office as well.

Finally arriving in her cold office, Josie sighed, opened her tiny window to let in the sun and got serious. She'd eaten an apple and a piece of toast. She was relaxed, rested and ready to get some work done. All hail the grand, conquering treasurer.

She pulled up the latest cut of Grand Springs budget on her computer, ready to jot down some notes.

She wondered what she should wear tonight. It would depend on the restaurant, of course. She had one slinky black dress that could probably widen Stryker's eyes. But maybe slinky was bad. Had Marjorie been slinky? What the hell had this Marjorie person looked like and why had she hurt a good man like Jack? The fool.

Josie blinked her eyes several times and realized she still hadn't taken any notes. She shook out her arms and crossed her legs in her official "I am working seriously" position.

She would wear her periwinkle silk sweater with her long flowered skirt. Elegant but feminine, and people always told her periwinkle did wonders for her eyes. She would wear that deep blue hair band, with her hair streaming down her back.

Yeah, and look sweet sixteen and never been kissed.

She never should've bought a floral skirt. What kind of an accountant wore a floral skirt? That was it. She was wearing her short black skirt with a white silk blouse with French cuffs and a long gold pendant. Elegant but sexy, alluring but not overdone. Classic. She'd pull her hair back in a twist.

She looked back at the rows of numbers. Okay, the women's shelter needed an additional twenty percent to build the annex. The police department's budget was to be increased ten percent to cover the hiring of two additional officers. Schools wanted twenty percent. Sanitation workers were threatening to strike if they didn't get a five percent cost-of-living raise across the board. Of course, no city officials wanted to raise taxes. So, treasure extraordinaire, find the extra 2.5 million dollars padding the budget and tell the good old city officials how they can make everyone happy without raising taxes or making a single compromise.

Oh, yeah, and teach pigs to fly.

What if Jack took her to a corner diner? A woman couldn't very well wear a short black skirt and silk blouse to a diner. He was a cop, a detective in a medium-size operation. He couldn't exactly afford Randolphs. What kind of restaurant did he have in mind?

And was he thinking of her right now, the way she was thinking of him? Was he replaying every detail of their impromptu evening together, over and over in his mind?

Or were the bright rays of the sun waking up his common sense and telling him how futile and silly it would be to date a woman like her?

She abandoned her computer screen, studying her phone instead. She willed it to ring. *Call me, Jack. Just touch base right now. You'll sound excited to see me, I'll be happy you're excited to see me, we'll both feel good. You can tell me what restaurant, I'll know what to wear and feel reassured. Afterward, I might even get some work done.*

The phone didn't ring. Her office was silent. City Hall was silent. Only the sun warmed her back.

She tapped her pencil on the desk, contemplating the next logical step. She could call him. It was the nineties, she was an intelligent, capable woman. She didn't have to sit around waiting for the phone to ring. She would call. Then she'd settle down and get some work done.

Call and say what? Hiya, big boy, was it as good for you as it was for me? Oh, hey, I'm running to the pharmacy for new shampoo this afternoon. Anything I can pick up for you? Are you a thin, lubricated or ribbed kind of guy?

Oh, God, she was sitting alone in her office and already blushing. She dropped the pencil with a clatter. She was not cut out for this. Too late, she was hopeless about this.

She was sitting at her stupid desk in her stupid office and she was remembering every moment of him barging into her house. The way he'd backed her against the door. The way he'd said, ''I want you, Josie.'' The way he'd kissed her, the way he'd touched her, the way he'd made her feel so beautiful and attractive and desirable after years of quiet, sterile existence.

She thought of him, and her stomach constricted. She remembered the feel of his hand on her breast, the darkening of his eyes, the hoarseness of his voice, and every damn nerve ending in her body began to quiver.

Oh, for God's sake, she was an idiot. She picked up the phone and dialed.

"Detective Stryker, please." She struggled to sound normal but only succeeded at breathlessness.

"I'm sorry, ma'am, but he's out of the office."

"What?"

"He's stepped out, ma'am. Would you like to leave a message?"

"Uh...I mean, no. It's all right. I'll call back later."

"Thank you, ma'am. Have a good afternoon."

Josie recradled the phone with a frown. She picked up the pencil and resumed rapping against her desk. Maybe he was at the pharmacy. Maybe he was standing in an aisle right now trying to figure out if she was a thin, lubricated or ribbed kind of woman. It would be worth asking him just to watch him blush again.

She sighed and reined in her riotous thoughts. Everything would be all right. He'd promised one step at a time. She could handle one step at a time. And if things continued to progress, maybe there would be a day when she could tell him about her father as she'd finally told Olivia about her father. And if he really cared for her, then he would understand as Olivia had understood.

One step at a time.

She turned back to her monitor. She got to work.

She didn't resurface until four o'clock, when she heard the ringing of footsteps on the hall corridor. She frowned, wondering what other fool would be in City Hall on a bright, sunny day. Then, as the footsteps approached her door, her stomach abruptly lurched and her head bobbed up.

Jack.

He knew she was coming into work. Maybe he really was as excited and nervous as she was. Maybe he'd decided to see her in person instead of just calling. Maybe he'd even brought her flowers. No one had ever brought her flowers. She'd always secretly, hungrily longed for a man to bring her flowers as her father had brought small bouquets of wild daisies and briar roses for her mother.

The footsteps stopped outside her door. The anticipation shivered through her, potent and sexual, more powerful than the short, tense storm that tingled up her spine right before the first kiss.

So help her God, if that was Jack, she was going to seduce him in her office just so she could breathe again.

The knocking on her door was polite, the voice unmistakable. "Josie Reynolds? It's Detective Stryker."

Jack!

She scrambled out from behind her desk with more haste than dignity. A silly, nervous grin wired her smile. She jerked the door open hard enough to yank it off its hinges.

"Hi!" she said breathlessly.

Sure enough it was Jack, more handsome than any man deserved to be in a dark gray suit, and yes, a spray-starched white shirt. He even wore one of those maroon ties with discreet blue diamonds. She never would've guessed that such a conservative, Republican tie would make her go weak in the knees.

God, she wanted to throw herself in his arms and kiss him until his perfectly groomed hair and perfectly pressed suit looked as hot and bothered as she felt.

But then her gaze slipped to the right. Stone Richardson,

considerably more casual in slacks and a plaid shirt, stood next to his partner.

Euphoria dimmed. For the first time, her breath caught in her throat and wariness halted her smile.

"Can...can I help you?"

Jack's gaze seemed to be locked somewhere behind her right ear. He held out the folded paper expressionlessly. "Josie Reynolds, we have a search warrant for your house. We would like you to come with us."

"Wh—what?"

"Josie Reynolds," he intoned again.

"Jack! What the hell is going on here!"

Stone shifted uncomfortably. "Josie," he began quietly, reaching out a soothing hand.

She jerked back from him, her eyes locked on Jack's remote gaze. "What the hell is going on, Stryker?"

"Some new evidence has come to light, Ms. Reynolds. We now have a search warrant for your house and car, all the paperwork is in order. Please come with us."

"What?"

"The search warrant—"

"What the hell, Stryker? You crawled out of my bed just five hours ago—"

Stone flinched, but she continued right on, too hurt and angry to care. "Flowers too traditional for you, Stryker? Is that it? So you serve me with a search warrant, instead? Well, not that I don't just adore such romantic overtures, but for future reference, I prefer daisies and briar roses."

Jack's jaw tightened, a muscle spasm visible in his cheek. He finally looked at her, then flicked his gaze toward his partner. "Not here. Not now," he warned quietly.

"Oh, I'm sorry. Please excuse me for embarrassing you. I've never been semiarrested by a man who'd just invited me to dinner and a night of endless passion. I imagine I have to work on my protocol."

"Josie…" His voice trailed off. For one moment, his eyes darkened. He looked angry. He looked frustrated. He looked betrayed. Then he shook his head and his face shuttered once more. "Please come with us, Ms. Reynolds."

His fingers folded around her elbow. His eyes were blank, his grip impersonal. And then she understood how totally he'd withdrawn from her. Her throat thickened. Her eyes filled with tears, and it took her a moment to breathe through the knot in her chest.

"Damn you, Jack Stryker," she cursed him thickly. "Damn you."

He simply pulled her down the hall, Stone falling in on her other side. The ceiling was high above them, the shadows long. Their footsteps rang hollowly, making her feel even more alone. She kept her head up proudly and she blinked the tears away. She would not give them that kind of satisfaction, not even when they opened the door of the squad car and guided her into the back seat.

She wondered if this was how her father had felt when they led him away. And she wished she'd never met Jack Stryker.

Stone Richardson spared another sharp glance over at his partner. Jack sat perfectly straight in the front of the squad car. His knees were together, his hands at his side, and his gaze locked straight ahead. No emotion or expression had crossed his face for the last three hours, not since Stone had opened a small package addressed to himself and found inside every detail of Josie Reynolds's life, downloaded from a computer service. A typed, unsigned note had been clipped to the front.

Dear Detective:
Jo Reynolds is not who she appears to be. Olivia found out the truth, look what happened to her.
Sincerely,
Someone Who Knows Better

Stone had quickly scanned the materials, then given them to Jack to read before sending the whole package to the lab to be analyzed for fingerprints. He hadn't understood why his partner had become so cold and remote until they went to pick up Josie. So Jack had spent the night with their number one murder suspect.

God, what a mess. And how totally unlike Straight Arrow Stryker.

"You should've let me handle it," he said under his breath to Jack. Josie wasn't paying any attention to them. Separated by bulletproof glass, she was hunched next to the locked back door, staring out the window and looking as miserable as Jack.

"I wanted to handle it."

"You could get into a lot of trouble for this."

"She wasn't the number one suspect last night."

"Dammit, Jack, play iceman with someone who doesn't know you as well as I do. You're involved with her. It's obvious you care. You should've let me handle it."

Jack turned to him at last. "I wanted to handle it. She shouldn't have been confronted by a stranger."

Stone grimaced and shook his head. "Stryker, one of these days, I'll have to teach you about women, because otherwise your sense of honor is going to get you killed."

Stone pulled into Josie's neighborhood. Two other squad cars were there. The warrant listed the whole house, garage and car as fair game. They had four officers to help search, with him and Jack overseeing the operation. It would probably take a few hours. Depending on what they found, they might have probable cause to get a new search warrant for Josie's office.

Stone pulled into the driveway, not bothering to get Josie from the back, but leaving her for his partner to handle. Once on the front porch, a pale and dry-eyed Josie stood quietly while Jack retrieved the door keys from her purse and opened it for all the officers.

"Why don't you take Ms. Reynolds into the kitchen," Stone told Jack brusquely.

"One of the other—"

"Why don't you take Ms. Reynolds into the kitchen?" Stone smiled more tightly. The search would start in the living room, then the bedroom, where personal items were more likely to be found. The kitchen would be the only place to give Jack and Josie the privacy he was sure they needed.

After a moment, Jack conceded with the smallest tilt of his head.

"Stubborn ass," Stone muttered. He started barking orders, and as Jack led Josie away, the rest of them got to work.

"Can I at least get a glass of water?" Josie asked at last. She stood in the middle of her own kitchen, uncuffed but feeling very much a prisoner. She didn't want to be alone with this man. She never wanted to look at him again.

"Where are your glasses?" He sounded as if he were talking to someone he barely knew, much less liked.

"Upper right cupboard. Afraid that's where I stash all my assault weapons?"

He wordlessly pulled down a glass, ran cold water in the faucet and filled the glass. He handed it out to her. She shook her head.

"There's bottled water in the fridge."

Not batting an eye, he dumped out the tap water, opened the refrigerator and refilled the glass. This time, he set it down on the counter, probably so he wouldn't have to risk brushing her fingers.

"You are such a bastard," she said at last. She was having to blink back tears again.

He pulled out a chair and sat. He locked his gaze on the far wall, and her blood boiled over.

"So that's it? I get the silent treatment now? At least I fight fair, Stryker. At least I say what's on my mind. You make the queen of England seem loose-lipped and wild."

"You're not as open as you pretend." His voice carried an edge. Fool that she was, she went after it.

"Yes, I am, Stryker. I'm exactly who I say I am. And when I said I was willing to take things one step at a time, I meant it. I meant I'd give you the benefit of the doubt. I meant I'd spend my afternoon looking forward to our evening together. I meant I honestly wanted to see you again and…and make more microwave popcorn!"

"And tell me lies, Josie? Lie in bed with me and tell me more lies?" He looked right at her and his blue eyes burned black.

"I never lied," she retorted immediately.

"*Dammit, how can you say that?* You told me your parents were perfect together. You spun golden stories of their incredible love and the tragedy of losing them both to an accident. An accident? Your father went to jail for murdering your mother. What kind of accident was that? And what kind of example of incredible love?"

"He didn't kill her."

"He didn't kill her? Funny, twelve jurors seemed to think differently."

"Oh? Why don't you ask a defense lawyer just how smart twelve jurors can be. My father didn't do it, Stryker. I know. I found her body."

He stuttered. His eyes narrowed, but she didn't look away. She furiously blinked away more tears, hating the thickness of her voice and the unbearably tight feeling in her chest. She wasn't a stranger to standing alone. She was a helluva lot tougher than Jack Stryker would ever understand. He could toy with her, he could hurt her, but she had no intention of ever letting him see her cry.

"Maybe you ought to start at the beginning, Josie. Maybe you ought to tell me what you should've told me last night."

"I didn't lie to you."

"Bull—"

"I did not lie to you, Jack Stryker. Now, are you going to shut up and listen, or are you going to continue to doubt me because that's what you do best?"

His jaw tightened dangerously. "God, Josie," he muttered through clenched teeth at last, "you could drive a Buddhist to murder."

"Thanks, it's a gift." She leaned back against the counter, crossed her arms over her chest and trapped him with her hot, angry gaze. "All right. I'll go through this once, that's it. Because, frankly, it's my family's business, not yours and not Grand Springs's."

"I think a lot of taxpayers would disagree with that—"

"Well, Olivia didn't. She considered it my business."

"So Olivia did find out."

"Of course she found out, Jack. I told her."

"What?"

"This would go a lot smoother if you would stop interrupting. Didn't anyone ever tell you that nine-tenths of good police work was being a good listener?"

He scowled. She smiled sweetly, but it didn't meet her eyes. She felt amazingly raw and amazingly brittle.

"My father, Stan Reynolds, loved my mother, Rose, just like I told you. And she loved him. My father wasn't perfect, but he had a good heart. He was just…he was a dreamer. He wanted to make it big, he wanted to build a castle in the sky for my mother. He hadn't the skills, but he thought he had the cleverness. He was a con man, all right? He was a warm, foolish, petty con man who wouldn't have hurt a flea—''

''Just bilk old women out of their retirements.''

''Are you telling this story, or am I? No, my father never 'bilked old ladies.' Part of being a good con artist is never taking anyone for more than they can afford to lose. If you take too much, the financial burden forces them to go to the police in order to recover the money. If you only take their 'extra,' well…most times they're too embarrassed by their own lack of judgment to report anything.''

''How convenient.''

''I'm not saying it was right, Jack. God knows my mother pleaded with him to go straight. For a while, he would try, wanting to make her happy. But my father didn't have any formal education or training. He only qualified for low-paying jobs like salesman or bartender. The work was boring, the pay not great, and Stan…Stan had too many dreams. Sooner or later, he'd hatch some great scheme, quit his job and get back in the game. Yes, he often involved me to give him credibility. Who could doubt a big, teddy-bear-looking man with a little girl?'' She paused, shrugging, but then added softly, ''He used to tell me, 'People need rainbows to chase, darlin'. They need to believe in that pot-o-gold, and you and me, we're just the little leprechauns helping them spin their dreams.'

''Of course, my mother always found out. Generally, when the police came to the house to question my father. God, it hurt her. She would stand in the kitchen, shaking his big shoulders as if he were a little child. 'How can I love you so much?' she'd cry, 'when you break my heart so often?'''

Josie's throat grew too tight. She took a deep breath so she could continue. ''The scams were always small stuff.

Sometimes they didn't have enough proof to prosecute. Sometimes he'd be found guilty and serve small time, or community service. He'd go straight for a bit. Life would settle down. He really loved my mother very much. He just kept thinking she deserved so much more than a little rental in a little community.''

"So he'd go back to scamming people." Jack's voice was hard.

"Yes," she said bluntly. "He would."

"And you would help him."

"I was a kid. He was my father. Of course I helped him."

"And now you control the town's money."

She stiffened, the blow cutting her deeper than she would've thought possible. She understood strength now. Strength was remaining standing against the counter and staring a man like Jack Stryker in the eye.

"Yes, Jack. And now I'm town treasurer. And as you should know from talking to all the people you've talked to, I'm really damn good at my job and I take it seriously. I'm sure you did a couple of things when you were ten that you wouldn't do as a cop now. Oh, wait, I take that back. You're Straight Arrow Stryker. You've never made a mistake. Too bad your brother isn't here, maybe he would understand.''

Jack went pale. She'd struck back unconsciously, but she'd struck deep. He'd hurt her. She'd hurt him. Suddenly, the ugliness of it all wearied her. She couldn't look at him anymore. She bled on the inside, and she just wanted to find a nice, dark place where she could curl up and lick her wounds. They had had only one night of closeness together, but she had liked it. The knowledge she'd never have it again salted the pain.

"Shall I continue?" she whispered.

"Might as well."

"Yeah, might as well." Her gaze went out the window. The sun was beginning to set, and the distant sky had turned gold and bloodred. "One day when I was twelve, my father confided in me that he had the scam to end all scams. This one would be the ultimate pot of gold. We'd retire afterward and build my mother a beautiful house. We would never want for anything. We would always be happy. I just had to come around with him a few days. He would help me make up the schoolwork later. Oh, and I absolutely, positively, should not tell my mom.

"I'd been around the block a few times by now. I listened to him describe the scheme that had been pitched to him by a man named Frank Gucci, and I recognized that it was a traditional Ponzi scam. We would approach people to invest and, as we got new investors, use their money to pay dividends to the first wave of investors, increasing credibility and thus gaining an even larger third wave of investors."

"You pay out dividends," Jack filled in, "while pocketing the serious investments. Everyone thinks it's legitimate because they are seeing some returns, while you get rich off the continual influx of money."

"Yes. Dad had played around with something like it before, but on a very small scale. Now he was talking of asking for investments in the tens of thousands of dollars. This guy Frank had dreamed it all up, setting up the shell as an investment fund in small-cap companies. It was a piece of cake. They just needed Dad as the front man, to actually approach potential investors. He was very charming and benign, not a sinister bone in his body. Women loved him."

She had to close her eyes. She loved her father dearly, but that didn't mean she approved of him. And yet the memories hurt, because she saw his laugh and his smile and the times he'd sneaked her oatmeal cookies. Her happiest times had been on his knee, and then everything had blown apart.

"To make a long story short, I told my mother what was going on. I was scared for him. The other stuff had been small and the risk small. This was the big league, with millions of dollars at stake, but also the potential to go to federal prison for wire and interstate mail fraud—"

"Among other things," Jack said dryly.

"Exactly. So I told, and two days later when I returned home, I found my mother's dead body at the foot of the stairs. Moments later, my father walked in. If…if you could've seen the look in his eyes, Jack. So much horror. So much pain. I'll never forget that look." Her voice grew soft. "I'll never forget what I did to my parents."

Her gaze swung to him slowly. "They killed her, Jack. Frank and his friends were afraid she'd go to the police, and this wasn't small-time stuff. They killed her because I told, and my father cradled her head on his lap and begged her to come back to life for him, not to leave him. He begged her to stay.…"

I'm so sorry, I'm so sorry, I'm so sorry.

She blinked back the tears. It didn't help. "My…my, uh, father left. We both knew the police would arrest him. He had a rap sheet. He was always questioned for the local crimes, regardless of involvement or not. So he left and I sat there until the police arrived."

"But they caught him," Jack filled in. "They arrested him, anyway."

"Eight months later," she said. "He just walked into police headquarters and said, 'I think you want me for murder.' He didn't look like Stan anymore. He was old and worn and so thin his clothes hung on him. They booked him for murdering my mother immediately and he didn't fight it. When I was finally allowed to visit him in jail, he told me not to worry about anything. It was his fault my mother had died, his fault because he should've gone straight as he'd always promised her. He told me I'd be better off without him.

"I begged him to fight the charges, of course. I told him we could live together, just him and me. We'd be all right. He just kept shaking his head. He went to prison. I was sent to live with the Brattles.

"Six months later, I saw the news report on the discovery of a body. A man named Frank Gucci had been pulled out of a pond. He'd been shot to death. He had a reputation for money laundering and racketeering."

She looked at Jack squarely. "My father would never tell me, but I believe to this day that he shot Frank Gucci. He'd gotten justice his own way, but at a huge price. My father wasn't meant to be a murderer, Jack. When my mother died, something inside him gave up. He'd done what he felt he'd had to do, but it hadn't made anything right. He died shortly after in prison. He didn't eat. He didn't fight. He just withered away.

"So yes, my parents loved each other. Yes, they died when I was twelve, because when my mother died, she took my father with her. Yes, it was accidental, because my father never would've done anything to intentionally harm my mother. And no, it has nothing to do with my job or respectability or character now. My father was a con man, Jack, but not me. My father shot a man. Not me. I grew up hard. I learned right from wrong by watching it play out in front of my eyes. I paid my way through college, I passed the CPA exam. And I moved to Grand Springs, where I have been one hell of a city treasurer, and Olivia Stuart became a second mother to me. I told her the truth about my past six months into this job, just in case she had doubts. She told me we all make mistakes, but we all learn and move on. She certainly didn't feel it was an issue. She believed in me."

Her tone very clearly implied that this made Olivia Stuart superior to Jack Stryker. He was quiet for a moment. His expression was turbulent. Abruptly, he dragged his hand through his hair.

"I don't know," he said curtly. "You do spin a good story."

"Oh, yes, that's what I like to do, Stryker. Mess with your mind."

"Well, you're doing one hell of a job at it." He looked at her fiercely. "Dammit, Josie, I did enjoy last night. I did mean it when I said I wanted to see you again. I went to work this afternoon, and even Stone said he'd never seen me smile so much. Then suddenly he's shoving this stack of papers under my nose, and I'm reading about how the woman I spent the night with had a con man for a father who murdered her mother. For God's sake, Josie, I'd just heard you tell me how in love they were with each other. How do you think that made me feel?"

"I don't know," she said tightly. "But maybe you could've asked me about it."

"I can't just ask you about it. I'm a cop."

"Well, I didn't kill Olivia Stuart, and I can't believe you people are searching my house because of something my father did twenty years ago. How is that probable cause?"

"There's more to it than that." He wouldn't look at her again.

"What do mean by that?" she demanded.

"I'm not at liberty to discuss the investigation with you. But as a detective, I can recommend that you call a lawyer."

She stared at him a moment, then she closed her eyes and shook her head. "Dammit, Jack, can't you trust me at all?"

"I…I don't know."

"God, you spent the night with me. Do you really think I could kill someone?"

He looked away. She could see that he was struggling as much as she was. "I want to believe in you, Josie," he said at last. Her elation, however, was short-lived. His gaze returned to her steadily. "But I can't."

"Jack—"

Stone abruptly walked into the kitchen. He looked at Josie, and she saw hurt and condemnation in his eyes. She felt as if she were in a dream, sucked into the Twilight Zone, and roaring filled her ears. What now? *What now?*

Stone held up a syringe and a vial. "We found the syringe in your bedroom, Josie. Along with the vial labeled Pure Potassium. Ms. Reynolds, you have the right to remain silent…"

She began to sway. Her gaze went to Jack. His expression had gone cold. As she watched, he reached behind him and pulled out the handcuffs.

"Anything you say can be used against you in a court of law. You have the right to an attorney—"

"This, this is ridiculous," she whispered hoarsely. "Why would I do such a thing? Jack…"

"We'll have to audit Grand Springs's books. Maybe they'll reveal the truth."

She recoiled. And the pain was too much. She wanted her mother, she wanted her father, she wanted Olivia Stuart back. She was so lost and there was no one to save her. Once more, a Reynolds was being thrown into jail and there was nothing she could do. And Jack Stryker wouldn't meet her gaze.

She stood alone and the weight crushed her to the floor, where the linoleum felt cold against her cheek right before the kitchen went black.

Seven

Some days just keep getting worse.

They drove Josie to the police station in silence. An officer took her fingerprints and police photo, then removed all her jewelry and put it in a manila envelope. She was handed an orange snap-up suit, official attire of the Grand Springs jail. Then they brought her to interrogation room B. The syringe and clear glass vial had gone to the state labs for analysis; they probably wouldn't have results back until at least Monday afternoon, but that didn't mean they couldn't question her about the articles now.

"Want to tell us one more time where that syringe and vial came from?" Stone did the talking. Jack wasn't sure he could get his lips to move.

"I don't know."

"Come on, Josie. This will go a whole lot easier if you just cooperate."

She looked at him flatly. "Gonna beat it out of me next?"

"Josie—"

"I want my attorney."

"Sure, sure, in a minute. Why don't you tell us where you got the potassium from. What about your pharmacist boyfriend?"

"I want my attorney."

"And the syringe? Did you get the syringe from him, too?"

She pursed her lips together and stared back mutinously.

"Why?" Stone asked softly. "Why did you kill Olivia Stuart?"

"Detective, give me my phone call now, or the civil suit will keep you tied up in court until you're ninety and Jessica will get to raise your children alone. Are we clear?"

They gave up and led her to the phone. It was a high-profile arrest —they couldn't afford any stupid breaches of protocol. Cases like this were strictly by the book.

After Josie disappeared down the corridor to her jail cell, Stone and Jack went to meet with Chief Sanderson. He was at once proud and nervous about the arrest. He'd known Josie. He'd liked her, but not all criminals looked like Satan. With them in his office, he called the mayor and informed him of the news. The chief would prepare a statement for the press, but of course they'd want one from the mayor's office as well. The chief looked them in the eye.

"You had a warrant?"

"Yes, sir."

"It was a clean search?"

"Yes, sir."

"You Mirandized her?"

"Yes, sir." Stone grinned. "Come on, chief, would we ever do anything wrong?"

Sanderson rolled his eyes. "This isn't fun and games, Richardson. You just arrested our city treasurer, for God's sake, someone who's been very active in the community—"

"Chief, she had potassium and a syringe taped beneath her bureau—"

The chief held up his hand. "I'm not saying she didn't do it. I'm just saying we'd better have all our ducks in a row."

"Ducks are in a row, sir, and quacking nicely."

They were dismissed in time to meet up with Josie's lawyer, a local guy Jack recognized from various functions. He didn't look amused.

"You the arresting officers?"

"Yes, sir." Stone was still talking, Jack still staring at far walls.

"Well, let me be the first to tell you that it will be a cold day in hell before you'll be allowed to question my client again. I've already read your case and it's so damn circumstantial any five-year-old could see she's innocent. Do you even know everything Josie Reynolds has done for this community? And now you're going to tell this town she's a murderer?" He shook his head. "Detectives, start eating your bran flakes, because I'm going to be all over you on this one."

He pivoted sharply and rapped down the hallway.

Stone took a deep breath, his glib expression falling away to reveal the strain underneath. "Nice guy," he muttered. "For a lawyer."

Jack remained leaning against his desk, his ankles crossed, his arms crossed, his face expressionless. Since he'd first seen the articles on Josie's father, a cold fist had formed in the pit of his stomach. Now it moved up to his chest, snatching the emotion from him and leaving him on autopilot.

Stone ran his hand through his hair. "Damn," he said at last.

Jack just nodded. There was a rare awkwardness between him and his partner. He didn't have the energy to bridge it.

"Chief's not going to be happy to hear that you were involved with her," Stone murmured.

"No."

"Anyone else know about it?"

"I didn't tell anyone."

"What about her? She tell people?"

Jack shrugged. He didn't want to think about Josie. He didn't want to remember her sprawled on her bed in her red kimono, smiling so purely. He didn't want to remember himself sitting in her kitchen, wanting to believe her so badly. "I don't know."

"Jack...you did what you had to do."

"Yeah. I'm good at that."

Stone sighed. "For the record, I never thought it would be her. I really...I really believed she was close to Olivia."

Jack didn't say anything. His eyes stung and he resented that. Dammit, he'd been ready to believe Josie, too. He'd wanted, he'd *needed* to believe her. His lips twisted, but the expression couldn't be called a smile. His gaze remained unfocused on the far wall as his thoughts grew fangs and quietly ate him alive.

First Marjorie and then Josie—he could really pick 'em, that's for sure. How could one man be so smart and objective about so much, and then show such horrible judgment toward women?

"You don't trust anyone, do you, Stryker?"

"There you are." Hal bustled through the door, looking like the chief's call had pulled him away from a party at the tennis club—he was wearing khakis, a polo shirt and leather loafers. "I heard you finally made an arrest in my mother's case."

"Josie Reynolds," Stone supplied. His tone was cool.

"What? Josie?" Hal seemed genuinely surprised. Then he simply shrugged. Abruptly, however, the full impact of the arrest hit him and his features screwed into a petulant scowl. "Ah, God, what a mess. She's city treasurer, you know."

"We know," Stone said dryly. "Look, we found a syringe and vial in her house. Lab results aren't back yet, but the case looks pretty tight."

"Huh." Hal was frowning, his political mind whirling. "She handles everyone's money. They're not going to like that. Did she say she was skimming from the books or something like that?"

"Ms. Reynolds has declined answering our questions. We would recommend an audit of the treasurer's office."

"Well, of course! First thing Monday, I'll make the call. Damn." Hal shook his head. "People aren't going to like this, it really makes the mayor's office look bad. I always wondered about her, too. I mean, anyone as beautiful as her, working as an accountant?" Hal shook his head again.

Jack discovered he wanted to hit the man. He clenched his fist at his side, he kept his face remote. But the fist was uncurling in his chest, his emotions churning to life. He was thinking of Hal's words and the press conference to come. Josie would be raked over the coals, personally and professionally. Just last week, everyone was telling him how good she was at her job, how much she gave to the community.

By next week, how many people would still stand behind her? And how many would simply shake their heads and write her off even before the trial? She had no family here, she had no best friends. Her boss seemed willing to hang her out to dry. Either way, her career was ruined.

She's a murderer, Jack. You were there to see the evidence. Stop playing the fool.

But he kept remembering the proud look on her face when he'd told her the town spoke highly of her. He recalled the patient way she'd helped Mr. Chouder and her passion for rebuilding after the storm.

Those impacts were real, those results meaningful. Josie Reynolds had given something to this town. And most likely, it would mean nothing now.

"I didn't kill Olivia, you idiot. She was like a second mother to me!"

"I'm going home now," he said abruptly. Hal had already walked away, but Stone looked at his partner with open concern.

"You wanna talk?"

"I want to get a good night's sleep."

"All right, all right. You could take tomorrow off, too, you know. I'll follow up with the arrest reports, but there's not much more to write up until the lab results come in."

"No, that's fine. I have other things to catch up on."

"It's a clean arrest," Stone said softly. "It's hard, but at least you found out the truth now."

"Yeah. I guess there's that."

Jack walked away without looking back. He drove home with his hands locked on the wheel, his mind too numb to think. His dark apartment offered no comfort. The musty, foreign smell had never faded after all these years; it still wrinkled his nose and made him feel like he'd entered a hotel. He decided against turning on a light, sitting in the darkness instead where he could pretend his apartment was more attractive, more cheerful than it really was.

He kept seeing Josie. Over and over again, standing in her kitchen, telling him about her parents, making him want to believe. God, he'd wanted to believe.

Stone walking in with the damning evidence. Her gaze turning automatically to him, pleading, beseeching…hurt.

Jack pinched the bridge of his nose with his index finger and thumb. He squeezed his eyes shut, but it didn't help. She was sitting in the county jail now, wearing an orange suit. Damn, damn, damn.

What was he supposed to believe? What was he supposed to believe?

He finally fell asleep. He dreamed of Josie, reaching out to him from behind prison bars. She begged him to help her, told him he was her last chance. No one had ever believed in her. No one had ever truly loved her. Couldn't he see the truth? Couldn't he trust her the way she had trusted him?

"One step at a time, Jack. You promised, you promised."

He gave in abruptly, reaching for her hands, trying to pull her into his arms. Then suddenly she was Marjorie, spiteful eyes laughing, dark hair tangling around him. He tried to yank back, but she held him in place as her hair turned into a nest of vipers and bit his hands.

By Monday morning, word was all over town. Josie Reynolds had been arrested for the murder of Olivia Stuart. The papers had a field day, the chief's phone rang off the hook. Judge Brennan was so impressed by the case, he denied her lawyer's request for bail, stating that the woman who'd spent three months rebuilding the town didn't have enough community ties to be a low flight risk. Now her lawyer was filing for a change of venue. According to him, there was no way Josie Reynolds would get a fair trial in Grand Springs.

Jack's father didn't disagree.

"What the hell have you done?" Ben demanded hotly by phone.

"Hi, Dad. Nice to hear from you, too."

"I tell you to ask a woman out on a date, and you arrest her instead? What were you thinking?"

"I was thinking that maybe I was still a cop."

"Cop shlop, any fool who knows Josie would know she'd never do such a thing. That woman loved Olivia. Didn't you see her face at the funeral? She was as distressed as Eve—"

"I would hardly expect a murderer to show up and gloat."

"And after everything she's done for this town! If it wasn't for her, old Bruester wouldn't have his new hay barn, Jimmy Eisinger wouldn't be able to feed his cows, and Simmons Hardware would've shut down for good after three generations of serving Grand Springs. Now, how do you explain a cold-blooded murderer doing all that?''

"Maybe she's gunning for the position of mayor."

"Mayor? Why would she want to be mayor? She's a damn fine treasurer and everybody loves her—"

"That doesn't mean she couldn't have further ambitions."

"Ambitions? Oh, for crying out loud, Jack, who would really kill to be mayor of *Grand Springs?* I love our community and all, but really, Jack, killing to be mayor of a small town? Start using your head, son, because Josie Reynolds is a real fine girl and there's no way she committed a murder. And next time I talk to you, I want to hear what you've done about all this!"

"Dad—"

Ben hung up in his ear. Jack replaced the phone with a sigh. And the call from his father had been one of the friendlier ones. The people who'd never worked with Josie Reynolds were willing to believe her guilty. But those who had were completely up in arms. A small fund was already being raised for her defense, and this from people who just two days ago were struggling to raise money for themselves.

Jack was stuck somewhere in the middle, one foot in either camp and feeling the strain. The cop in him couldn't ignore the evidence. The man in him couldn't forget holding her in his arms. Historically speaking, however, the cop part of Jack Stryker had shown much better judgment than the man part.

He didn't show up to work until 10:00 a.m. There he was greeted with the lab reports on the syringe and vial, as well as the mysterious envelope they had received containing the information on Josie. The envelope hadn't yielded fingerprints, saliva or a postmark. It had obviously been sealed and delivered by someone who knew what they were doing.

The syringe and the vial were also lacking fingerprints. The needle, however, had traces of Olivia Stuart's blood and skin. And the vial contained one hundred percent pure potassium.

"I brought you lunch."

Sitting on her stiff jail bed, Josie stiffened, fighting the urge to turn at the sound of Jack's voice. She'd been rotting in this damn jail cell for almost two days with only her lawyer, eager Edward Finnley, for company. Apparently, she was the only female criminal currently residing in Grand Springs, so most of the other cells in the women's section were empty. Of course, late Sunday night a couple of "professionals" had moved in briefly as next-door neighbors. They'd cracked their gum a lot, resigned to staying overnight because as they'd told her, their "men" wouldn't bother with them till morning 'cause it was their own damn fault for gettin' caught.

Mostly, however, Josie sat alone in the middle of a shadowed, cement world where the odors of cleansing fluid and urine rolled across the floor in a thick miasma, curling into her hair and tattooing her skin. She didn't remember what fresh air smelled like anymore, or how real clothes would feel. She got to pee staring at the corridor and hoping no one would walk by. The other two women hadn't appeared to be bothered by the lack of privacy, so maybe she would get used to it in time. For now, her shame had backed up her system to such a point that all the bran flakes in the world weren't going to help.

She wanted her house back. Her bedroom, her feather bed. She wanted her office and her dignity and her pride. She wanted the life she'd so carefully built, one brick at a time, so no one would ever doubt her or think of her as the Irishman's daughter.

"Honestly," Jack ventured again from the corridor, "I left my thumbscrews at home."

"Hah!" She figured if she could get her hands through the bars, she might be capable of murder, after all. She kept her back to him resolutely.

"You don't even want your lunch?"

His voice was cajoling. She granted him one look of pure disdain. "Sorry, but I don't like green eggs and ham."

She was rewarded by him shifting from foot to foot uncomfortably. His blue-striped shirt wasn't so sharply pressed this morning. Shadows marred his eyes, and his short-cropped hair was actually rumpled. So Jack Stryker was suffering a bit. Good.

"Josie—"

"Don't you have someone else to go frame?" She turned away as he recoiled. The tin lunch tray was set down with a clatter on the passing shelf.

"What exactly do you mean by that?" She heard the beginnings of temper in his voice. It filled her with despair and delight. She had always liked getting his goat—ruffling cool Straight Arrow Stryker. Watching his eyes darken as his gaze fell to her lips, watching his temper turn to other, more compelling emotions.

Now, what was the point?

"Josie, dammit, you can't just state allegations like that and then clam up!"

"Oh? What are you going to do, Jack? Arrest me?" She smiled sweetly and watched him count to ten, then drag a hand through his hair. She took back her earlier thought. She felt only delight. Tormenting Stryker was the first bit of enjoyment she'd had in days.

"I do not plant evidence," he said firmly. "And I resent that accusation."

"Oh, for heaven's sake!" She couldn't help herself. She clambered to her feet and crossed to the front of the small jail cell where she could glare at him up close and personal. He was wearing that tie again, the maroon one with little blue diamonds. And dammit, he looked sexy as hell in his dark gray suit. She clenched her fists at her side. "You resent that accusation? *You* resent that accusation? You've accused me of murder! How the hell do you think I feel?"

"Well, you had a murder weapon in your possession, Josie. I couldn't exactly tell you to run along after discovering a thing like that!"

"Exactly!" she fired back. She was close to him now, just the bars separating the heated exchange. "And since I know I didn't tape a syringe or bottle of potassium to the bottom of my bureau, I can only assume that one of you cops did!"

"What? Why would we do something like that? That's ridiculous!"

"I don't know. Why would I do something like kill my best friend? Now, that's ridiculous!"

"Josie, you cannot make such allegations," he warned darkly.

"Jack, you could not be denser about all this if you'd had a full frontal lobotomy!" She whirled away, too angry to continue. And her eyes stung again. She knew he was a cop, and cops were by definition low on imagination and cleverness, but his distrust still hurt, dammit. She didn't want to be hurt by him anymore. "Go away, Stryker. And don't come back unless you're ready to really listen."

"I came here to listen!" Abruptly, he scowled. Out of the corner of her eye, she caught him raking his hand through his hair again. That was twice in ten minutes.

She'd never seen him so distressed. "I'm yelling again, aren't I?" he asked finally.

"Trust me, officers on duty in Boulder have gotten to hear this conversation."

"Well, I don't usually yell. That's not what I came down here for. You just…you have a way of provoking me, Josie, and we both know you do it on purpose so don't look so damn innocent."

"I wasn't looking innocent. I was looking smug."

"Oh, my God," he said in clear frustration. "You are trying to drive me to kill you."

"Frankly, Stryker, it's the only entertainment I have left." Her shoulders came down. She didn't mean to suddenly sound so defeated, but her own words depressed her. In the beginning, she'd thought this whole thing was a horrible misunderstanding, at worst a case of bias against her criminal father. But as Finnley had shown up with more and more updates, she'd begun to realize just how strong the case was against her. Maybe she'd even begun to understand why Jack would have trouble believing in her innocence. Someone was doing quite a number on her. And she had no idea who or why.

And no one to turn to for help.

"Go away, Jack."

"I can't."

"Yes, you can. You're Straight Arrow Stryker, Boy Scout extraordinaire. You can walk away from a murder suspect with no problem."

"Maybe, but my father would kill me."

"Really?" Now he had her attention. "Ben believes I'm innocent?"

"Ben believes the sun and moon rise and set at your feet. I, on the other hand—how did you put it?—couldn't be denser about this if I had a full frontal lobotomy."

"Your father," she assured him, "is a very smart man."

"He certainly thinks so." Jack regarded her steadily for a moment. "You know some of the people you helped are really on your side, Josie. They're gathering a defense fund for you and everything."

For a moment, she swayed on her feet. Edward Finnley hadn't told her this. No one had told her this. She'd spent the last forty-eight hours feeling unbearably alone. "R-r-really?" she whispered.

"Really," he said quietly.

She had to sit down. Her hands folded on her knees, she blinked back more tears. "That's…uh…that's really nice of them."

It was more than nice. It was the nicest thing anyone had ever done for her, and now she wanted to cry. In the dark solitude of her jail cell, Josie had discovered there was one thing in the world she wanted more than any other—to belong, to feel like she had a home, with neighbors and friends and peers who loved and respected her. For a while, she'd felt like she had that here. Then in a blink of an eye, it had seemed gone.

She finally risked looking at Jack. "Do you think they're crazy, Stryker?" she whispered thickly. "Are you telling me this because you hope it would make my conscience feel guilty enough to admit to murder?"

He shifted from foot to foot. "I don't know why I told you," he admitted roughly. "I just…I just wanted you to know."

"You do think I did it, don't you?"

"The evidence tells me that."

"Of course," she murmured. "Of course."

She turned away so he wouldn't see the first tear fall from her lashes. Had it been only three nights ago he'd shown up at her house, telling her how much he wanted her? Had it been only two days ago she'd slept curled up at his side, feeling warm and safe and happy?

She wanted him to go away now. No, she wanted him to tell her that he believed she was innocent. She wanted him to pull her into his arms and tuck her head against his shoulder. She wanted him to stroke her hair and whisper words of nonsense. Then she wanted him to kiss her until no more troubled thoughts filled her head.

"Josie—"

"If our positions had been reversed, Jack, I would've believed in you."

"You don't know that."

"Yes, I do. Because I'm willing to believe my gut, I'm willing to trust my instincts." *I'm willing to follow my heart.* She took a deep breath and lifted her chin. "I would've believed in you, Jack. And I'm not sure I can ever forgive you for not doing the same."

For a moment, he appeared uncomfortable, even ashamed. But then he determinedly shook his head. "Josie, we found the murder weapon taped to the bureau in your bedroom—"

"Why would a murderer keep incriminating evidence for three months, Jack? Better yet, why would she keep the evidence in her bedroom when a local cop was already sniffing at her heels and had spent a night in her room—"

"You didn't know I was coming over."

"I didn't exactly kick you out."

"But what were the chances of me looking beneath your bureau drawer?"

"But why didn't I at least get rid of it, then? We'd already talked about getting together in the evening. You...you were going to go to the pharmacy. Come on, Stryker, we both knew you were going to spend Saturday night at my place. Why would I even chance it?"

His brow crinkled into a frown. "Well, if you didn't put it there, who do you think did, Josie? Has anyone broken into your home recently?"

"Well...no."

"Does anyone have an extra key?"

"No." Her voice had gone soft and troubled.

"Has anything been out of the ordinary lately? Have you felt like you were being watched? Have things in your house been missing?"

She hung her head. "No," she admitted at last. "Nothing comes to mind. But—" she lifted her chin back up for battle "—that simply means the person was very, very good. Can't professionals pick locks? Would a layman notice?"

"Maybe. All right, all right," he amended, catching her look, "probably not."

"Did you fine, upstanding officers of the law examine my doors and windows for signs of tampering?"

He shook his head and she gained momentum. "Exactly. So you haven't done all your homework, either. Suppose for a moment I'm not the killer. Then, who would know my schedule? Actually—" her brow furrowed "—everyone would know when I was out because all the town's events are in the Community section of the newspaper, and I'm listed as head chairperson of most. So see, opportunity would be easy to come by. I don't have a sophisticated lock system or alarm system, so entry isn't that hard, either. I'm never home, we've both established that, and generally I'm home just in time to sleep. So there, it's pretty darn easy to frame me. Hah."

Jack didn't look convinced. "Those are a lot of assumptions."

"Welcome to real life."

"Oh, don't be so glib, Josie. I am listening, but police work isn't about assumptions. It's about facts. If you'd noticed anything awry, reported a break-in recently, then I could give your theory more credit—"

"Gardenias," she said abruptly. "When I came home

after the Band, Bingo, Bake Sale fund-raiser, I opened my bedroom window because I swore I kept smelling gardenias. I hate that scent, Jack. Last time I smelled it was when I found Olivia collapsed on her floor.''

Jack was very still. ''Gardenias?''

''Gardenias.''

His gaze seemed to have grown very watchful. ''You don't have any potpourri or floral perfume or candles or anything like that?''

Josie arched a brow. ''Heavy floral scents and me? Nice powers of observation from a cop.''

''Yeah, yeah, yeah. I had to ask.'' At least she'd finally etched uncertainty onto his brow. What was it about the scent of gardenias that bothered him so much? Abruptly, he squared his shoulders. ''You match the description of the woman we're looking for,'' he said doggedly.

She rolled her eyes. ''Yeah, Edward Finnley told me about this. With all due respect to Jessica, how much weight can you give a 'vision' of a tall, possibly blond woman dressed head to toe in black with long red fingernails. For her and Stone's sake I hope the D.A. doesn't intend to put her on the stand because Finnley would eat her alive.''

''Your name can be abbreviated to Jo. We have Randi's testimony that two men said, 'Jo will take care of the broad—it's her specialty.' ''

''Stryker, no one calls me Jo. And if I was going to bump someone off, wouldn't I at least use another name? How do you even know that statement had sinister intent—''

''They pursued Randi with pretty sinister intent when they realized she'd overheard it.''

''Maybe they just like to chase brides. I don't know. But I'm not Jo.''

Jack shook his head. ''If it were only one or two things,

Josie, maybe I could believe you. But you put them all together…''

''And Jack Stryker, who always gets his man, figures he's done it again,'' she filled in for him tiredly. ''Way to go, Jack.''

He didn't refute it and he didn't look away. She wanted to throttle him, she understood him too well. His unwavering principles at once attracted her to him and made her want to kill him.

She leaned forward, resting her elbows on her knees. She took a deep breath and gave it one last shot.

''Jack, how did I benefit from Olivia's death?''

''We're still looking into that.''

''So you have your theories?''

''A few.''

''Come on, Jack. Toss them out. Impress me with your brilliance. Tell me how I became better off by killing the woman who was a second mother to me.''

His jaw tightened. ''Maybe you wanted her job—''

''Mayor of Grand Springs? Hardly. But if I had, I imagine Olivia would've considered me a worthy successor.''

''Maybe you wanted it now.''

''I see. So risking a murder charge was smarter than waiting out another term and gaining increasing community recognition and goodwill. Geez, Jack, are all criminals so stupid?''

''Maybe you were afraid she'd tell people about your father.''

''She hadn't told anyone in a year and a half. Why would she tell someone now?''

''We have only your word that you told her anything. Besides, we're still auditing the town books.''

She winced, she couldn't help it. That accusation hurt her the worst, and they both knew it. Her reputation was shattered. Years of clean living and hard working eradicated just like that. Even if by some miracle she was found not guilty, people would always wonder. Town treasurers couldn't afford that kind of doubt.

Her career was over. Damn, and damn it all again. She was going to cry once more.

She hung her head, studying the scuffed-up floor of her cell while she fought for composure. "They won't find anything when they audit the books," she murmured at last. She knuckled her eyes. "I called the EMTs," she whispered hoarsely. "You would think a murderer wouldn't do such a thing."

"Pure potassium induces immediate cardiac arrest," Jack said quietly. "The murderer would know that and understand that calling the EMTs didn't matter—there is nothing they would be able to do."

"I see."

"Josie—" He gave up. Neither of them could take it anymore. "I'm going to go now. Your lunch is still here."

"Lucky me."

"If you need anything…"

"I'll call my lawyer," she supplied. "Because he's the only one here who believes in me."

Jack flinched, then turned and walked away. She didn't try to stop him.

Eight

Jack worked until the sun fell, the department calmed down and the reporters gave up and went home. Stone was out working on another case, which was just as well. Jack had too many conflicting thoughts to face Stone's perceptive questions. For now, he wanted time alone.

No, he wanted to stop thinking of Josie sitting in a jail cell.

A little after nine, Jack left. The night was cool, but not bad. Streetlights gave the city a friendly look, and a few other pedestrians wandered around. He nodded to them and they nodded back.

He kept walking until he found himself at Vanderbilt Park. Then he just stood, staring at the empty park bench. Eve Stuart liked to come here to sit. She'd told him once it was Olivia's favorite place. Now he stared at the fine wood-and-wrought-iron bench and willed it to speak to him.

"Rough night?"

Jack half bolted out of his skin before he realized the voice wasn't coming from the bench, but from the man walking up the pathway toward him. "I gotta get more sleep," he muttered to himself.

"I would think you'd be happy," the man said. "After all, you've finally made an arrest in Olivia's case."

The man stepped into the wash of the park lights and Jack instantly relaxed. It was Martin Smith, Grand Springs's resident John Doe. He'd been found almost four months ago, during the storm and power outage, wandering the mountain roads alone with a lump the size of a baseball on his forehead. He had no memory of his name or where he'd come from and carried no ID. For almost four months, he'd stayed in Grand Springs, trying to find some clue to his identity. Jack and Stone had researched it all they could, but neither Martin's face nor fingerprints had yielded any information.

At six-three, with intense blue eyes and a lean, rugged build, Martin at least wasn't lacking in companionship. Most single women in Grand Springs were dreaming up the man's future for him, regardless of his absent past. Every town needed a mystery man, and the women of Grand Springs thought Martin filled the bill quite nicely.

"How are you, Martin?"

"Just fine. Having a grand time cruising memory lane." His flashing smile was at once ironic and wry. "And you? Judging by your expression, I'd have to say, what's her name?"

Jack grimaced. "It shows that much?"

"Josie Reynolds," Martin said after a moment. For a man with no past or future, his blue eyes were clear, intelligent and knowing. "Tough arrest. A lot of people think very highly of her."

"Yes, there's that."

"I happened to notice you two together at the fundraiser. I would say you think rather highly of her, as well."

"Yeah," Jack said at last. "I suppose I did."

"Did or do?"

Jack shook his head. "Are you sure you weren't with the Gestapo, Martin? You have a flair for questions."

"Possibly. At this point, I could even be head of the Russian Mafia, controlling a vast empire of money, intrigue and murder. I might also be a poor idiot whose wife just ran out on him for the pool boy." Martin shrugged.

"I don't mean to pry, Stryker. I just have a habit of observing a lot of things, being the resident amnesiac—"

"You've been following Olivia's case," Jack filled in bluntly. "Stone and I know you've been pulling up a lot of things in the library on her."

Martin was silent for a moment. "Think I'm a suspect?"

"If I thought that, I would've hauled you in and questioned you. For now, we consider you someone who's just taken a great deal of interest in the case."

Martin frowned, nodding slowly. "Yes, the case does fascinate me. I wish I could tell you why, but I have no idea. Maybe I just have too much time on my hands. Maybe it's because Olivia died the day I appeared and I wonder if there might be some connection."

"Find anything?"

"No. Not at all. My own identity remains the biggest riddle."

"And what about Olivia Stuart's case? Want to lend your 'expert opinion' to an overworked detective?"

Martin smiled. "I don't think my expert opinion is worth that much. But since you asked, I don't think Josie did it."

"You've been talking to my father, haven't you," Jack murmured.

Martin took him seriously and shook his head. "Fundamentally, I think there's a problem of motive," he said immediately.

"Fundamentally?"

"Absolutely. They've been auditing the books all day, but I've been asking around and no one believes for a minute that Josie was skimming off the top. For starters, all the storm fund-raising money has been publicly accounted for. Other people worked on the committees and reported the money that came in. The farmers and businesspeople have confirmed receiving what the books said they received, so all that money is accounted for to the dime. It will take a bit longer to look at the entire Grand Springs budget, of course, but look at Josie's lifestyle. She lives in a modest neighborhood, drives an economy car and wears sensible clothes. If she was taking money, where does it go? Certainly she isn't stuffing her mattresses with it—you guys already searched her house. She doesn't party, travel or appear to have any gambling or drug habits. At least not that anyone knows of. Have *you* heard of any gambling or drug habits?''

"No," Jack admitted, intrigued by Martin's analysis. For a layman, he made a good cop.

"Then you have Josie herself. She's a smart woman, everyone agrees on that. Yet, you're saying the murderer was intelligent enough to research pure potassium, arrive at Olivia's when she was alone and inject a needle in a struggling woman. This same smart assassin then hung on to the syringe and drug for three months, with the detective in charge of the case visiting her home.''

"Josie makes the same argument.''

"And think of the injection spot itself," Martin continued, unperturbed. "Back of the knee. In Jessica's vision, she sees the woman in black come up behind Olivia, pinning a fighting Olivia in place with one arm while injecting her with her free hand. Face it, Josie would never have had to do that. Any of it.''

Jack's gaze narrowed. "Why?''

"Josie was Olivia's best friend. They were together all the time. Why wouldn't Josie just come over to Olivia's house dressed for the wedding? She could have the prepared syringe in her purse. She could wait until Eve left, then the moment Olivia turned away to do anything, simply stab the syringe in Olivia's upper arm, catching her off guard. The cardiac arrest would be immediate. Josie could recover the syringe, tuck it back in her purse, then call the

EMTs. She could just say she was talking with Olivia when Olivia clutched her heart, and 'boom.' Very simple. No one would question anything.''

"But if Olivia somehow lived, she could identify Josie.''

"Then, she waits until Olivia is dead, then calls the EMTs. Again, cause of death appears to be a heart attack. She would call less attention to herself that way than skulking around a house dressed in black and fighting with Olivia. No, I think Jessica's vision suggests Olivia was attacked by a stranger.''

Jack frowned. Martin raised some good points. Or maybe he was just telling Jack what Jack already wanted to hear. "What do you know about gardenias?'' he asked Martin abruptly.

"Gardenias?''

"Yes.'' Jack hesitated, then said slowly, "For some reason, gardenias keep popping up in this investigation. Josie said she smelled gardenias when she discovered Olivia's body. Someone sent a bowl filled with gardenias as a funeral arrangement. Friday night, Josie said she smelled gardenias in her bedroom when she returned from the fund-raiser.''

"Gardenias, gardenias, gardenias,'' Martin agreed. He was frowning, too. "Gardenias don't grow in Grand Springs. Did you try to trace the bouquet sent to Olivia's house?''

"They didn't come from a florist. They were hand-delivered without any card.''

"Don't all flowers symbolize something? Are gardenias peace? I can't remember.''

"I can't, either, but I could ask a florist.''

"What about the drug gangs or strip mining companies?'' Martin asked abruptly. "Now, there are two groups with motive. Do any of the gangs have a gardenia as a symbol?''

Jack raised a brow. ''Oh, sure. And the Bloods are about to turn in their bandannas for daisies.''

Martin chuckled. ''All right, dumb question.''

''But the strip mining companies,'' Jack mused. ''That's worth looking into.'' He studied Martin for a moment. ''You know, you're very good at this.''

''Almost a natural,'' Martin said dryly. ''Makes you wonder, huh?''

Jack nodded. ''You think like a cop,'' he said quietly. ''But if you were a cop, your fingerprints would've registered.''

''Yes. And they didn't. And no one recognized my picture, either, which you've posted all over hell and back. So I'm probably not a cop. On the other hand, I seem to know this stuff very well. Maybe I'm head of the Russian Mafia, after all.''

''You can always change. It's the advantage of amnesia. Your past is gone, a clean slate. Now you start again.''

''True.'' For a moment, Martin appeared tired and frustrated, then he simply shrugged. ''Then again, maybe I'd finally won the lottery. It would be a damn shame to lose those millions now, don't you think?''

''Good point. Well, good luck, Martin. And thanks for the conversation.''

''No problem. Good night, Detective.''

Jack walked away. The last time he turned around, he saw Martin sitting alone on Olivia's park bench, stroking the wood and gazing at the half-moon.

Tuesday morning, Jack pulled up in front of Josie's house. He called himself a fool several times, then gave up and climbed out of his car. No lights were on, of course.

The house was locked and silent and would be for as long as Josie was denied bail—or found guilty.

Jack didn't need to go inside the house, however. He just wanted to search the outside. He started with the back sliding glass door. No indents of footprints on the ground, no scratches around the lock. He moved to the windows, inspecting the ground, the casing, and then the glass. No footprints, no fresh cracks or chipped paint along the window edges, no fingerprints on the glass. Everything was locked up and undisturbed.

He examined the roof of the one-story house. The rim was slightly mossy from all the rain. Josie should have her gutters cleaned and replaced soon, he thought idly. Then his methodical mind turned to more important matters— any sign of trespassing on the roof. But the moss was a smooth, undisturbed green carpet.

Walking slowly, Jack returned to the front door. He almost couldn't bring himself to look at the lock. Would it be forced open or not? Would there be some evidence to back up Josie's allegations, or would he be back where he started from, wondering how he could want a woman so much when she'd most likely committed murder?

Straight Arrow Stryker. What had he done to get into this position? Why didn't his cool, rational mind carry over to his personal life, as well?

Why couldn't Josie be who he wanted her to be?

He looked at the lock. He studied the front door for twenty minutes. It did him no good.

He couldn't find any evidence of someone breaking and entering. None at all.

"Oh, look, it's the dynamic duo."

Stone turned to Jack as they walked down the corridor of the county jail. "Confinement hasn't done wonders for her temperament."

"Hey, I can still hear and think. You don't have to talk like I'm not even in the room. I'm in the damn room, all right! No one will let me go anyplace else." Josie almost rattled the bars of her cage in frustration, but having tried that earlier in the week, she knew by now that it didn't work the same way as in the movies. Those bars shook a little, giving a nice melodramatic flair. The bars of her jail cell, on the other hand, didn't budge at all. Colorado seemed to produce some mighty fine steel.

It was Wednesday morning now. Day five of the Great Fiasco as Josie had dubbed it in her mind. Five days of wearing orange jumpsuits and lying alone on her bed. Five days of eager Edward Finnley becoming less and less eager. Every day, he paid her a visit and brought her the slew of papers he was collecting for the change of venue hearing. The press dutifully reported all the evidence found in her house and the ongoing audit of the town records. Then the media had gleefully pursued any rumor, allegation or sighting of an alien spacecraft in Josie's backyard that it could.

"We're not ready to make a statement just yet," Hal Stuart had told the *Grand Springs Herald,* "but certainly every penny Josie Reynolds has ever touched is undergoing careful scrutiny. If there were any funny games with the town finances, we will catch them and, of course, action will be taken."

"I don't know," Eve Stuart was quoted as saying. "My mother considered Josie to be a second daughter. I would hate to think Mom was harmed by someone so close to her."

That quote was in an article calling Josie Grand Springs's very own Jezebel. Others carried quotes from anonymous "insiders" who reported Josie spent an undue amount of time at City Hall. They figured she was up to something a long time ago. After all, how many Saturdays did one public servant really need to work?

Josie had her supporters—Finnley said her defense fund had risen to five thousand dollars, and certainly Rio Redtree was raising some good questions in his articles for the *Grand Springs Herald*—but at this point, Josie figured the mob would arrive with torches and a rope by nightfall.

Yesterday, Finnley had explained the change of venue hearing to her. His mood had been the grimmest ever, and Josie had read between the lines all the things he wasn't telling her—the case against her was strong, the battle before them long.

Maybe even he wasn't quite so sure of her innocence anymore.

When he'd left, Josie had lain down, thinking she would cry. But she hadn't. There were no tears inside her anymore, just anger and frustration. Because she knew she hadn't done anything wrong, she knew she was being framed. And dammit, somehow she was going to get herself out of this, if she had to take on the whole state of Colorado to do it.

"We're to escort you to the courthouse," Jack said stiffly. She figured that meant he still considered her guilty. That probably hurt her the worst, though she wasn't sure why. She'd never actually spent much time with Jack Stryker. One night of passion hardly equaled deep and meaningful commitment. During the long nights, she consoled herself with the fact that they hadn't actually had sex. She hadn't quite given that much of herself to him. She hadn't quite been that big of a fool.

Now she delivered her grimmest smile to him and kept her chin in the air.

"Gonna search me first, Stryker? Oh, wait, male cops can't handle female suspects. Too bad we didn't think about that Friday night."

His jaw tightened, but his eyes didn't blink. She dug in her heels and prepared for out-and-out war.

"How's life on the outside, anyway? Eat any good doughnuts, boys? Frame any sweet old ladies? I'd hate for you to get bored."

"If we ignore her," Stone murmured, "maybe she'll tire and shut up."

Josie switched her disdainful glance to him. She'd liked Stone once. When he'd first questioned her about Olivia's death, his gaze had held honest compassion. Now she saw only remote professionalism in his gaze. She was the prisoner, and like Jack, Stone had tried her and found her guilty. One good fool deserved another.

"She doesn't shut up," Jack said. "She's right about the search, though. We need to get a female officer down here."

"Hang on." Stone walked to the end of the short corridor to call for a female cop. He didn't leave the area, because the stationed officer had already walked away, and as Josie had learned, a male cop wasn't allowed to be alone with a female prisoner.

Still, Josie leaned forward and said low enough for only Jack to hear, "Did you check out anything, Stryker? Did you at least grant me that much?"

"I checked things out, Ms. Reynolds." He looked her straight in the eye. "I didn't discover any signs of forced entry."

"What?"

"You heard me."

"But...but there had to be forced entry. Someone had to plant..." She rubbed her temples, even more frustrated and now also scared. Just who were these people and how good were they? Could they float in and out of houses like phantoms, or did they just have the funds to buy the stories they needed, or a good, old-fashioned cop like Jack? No, she dismissed that theory. Jack Stryker was too much of a stubborn mule to be bought.

"If they picked the lock, would you be able to see that?"

"There were no fresh scratches around the lock."

"Yes, but there would only be fresh scratches if they were harsh about it. A real pro...they could do it without leaving behind any marks, couldn't they? They'd manipulate the lock just as if they'd used a key."

"Josie, you've seen too many movies."

She opened her mouth to argue it further, but the end of the corridor slid open and the female officer arrived. She entered Josie's cell all business. Josie had gone through this drill before, too, but that didn't make it any easier.

She lifted her arms up into a T. She spread her legs. And she stood there like a human sacrifice, keeping her chin up even as her eyes burned with tears of humiliation. Jack and Stone appeared bored, like doctors with a patient. The female cop was equally quick and dispassionate. Josie wasn't, though. The thirty-second pat down seemed like an eternity to her, and in that time, she cursed Jack Stryker again because he'd brought her to this horrible place. Because he thought she deserved to be treated like this.

"She's clean," the female officer said briskly, already heading back down the corridor to the main police department.

"Oh, goody," Josie muttered, "she didn't find the lock pick I made from bent paper clips and tucked beneath my tongue."

"Jokes like that will earn you a body cavity search. Do you really want a body cavity search?"

Josie recoiled physically, appalled by Jack's suggestion and cool tone. "You are despicable!"

"I'm just doing my job."

"Yes, well, Torquemada probably thought the same!"

Jack ignored her. He took her arm, pulling her toward him. For a moment, she fought it. She was angry and she was frightened. And she would rather be alone than next to him again. He wore a navy blue suit and a red paisley tie. His hair was smooth, and he smelled of fresh air and clean soap. He was Jack Stryker, handsome, strong, and invincible.

And she didn't understand how he could've once held her so tenderly, then look at her as coldly as he did now. And she didn't understand how she could look at him and still want him. How she could look at him and still see the shadows beneath his eyes, the lines of strain on his forehead, and want to smooth them away.

I really liked you, Jack. I really, really did.

He and Stone flanked her sides. The three of them walked down the corridor. Outside, the reporters waited with cameras. Her lawyer had warned her about all this.

They came to the closed door. She could already hear the dull roar of pushing, prodding people, the clicking of cameras.

Town Treasurer on Trial! Reynolds Rapped for Murder!

Stone grabbed the door handle. "Ready?" His gaze was on Stryker.

There was a small pause. Suddenly, Josie felt Stryker give her arm a gentle squeeze. "Just keep your head low," he said quietly. "We'll get you through quickly."

She couldn't think of anything to say. Jack turned to Stone. "Ready," he said.

Stone opened the door and the lightbulbs began to flash.

Jack didn't relax until they pulled away from the police department and the media horde. He had a feeling the courthouse would be little better, and there was nothing to do but plow through.

Stone sat quietly beside him in the passenger's seat, looking grim and serious. It was a bright sunny day and the car was stifling for all three of them in their long-sleeved suits. Stone fiddled with the air-conditioning, then swore.

"Damn car pool. Just ensures that none of the vehicles work."

Jack tried the knob, as well. The air-conditioning was definitely out.

"The old-fashioned way," he said, and rolled down his window halfway. With more grumbling, Stone followed suit.

"What, you're not going to roll down my windows?" Josie called from the back. She added with saccharine innocence, "Don't you fellas trust me?"

Stone started to smile, of course. Jack gave his partner the sternest look possible, and the smile turned into a half-hearted cough.

"Don't encourage her," he said. "She doesn't need encouragement."

Stone nodded dutifully, but Jack's look wasn't nearly so effective on Josie. Sitting squarely in the middle of the back seat with her hair pulled back from her delicate, unmade-up features, she met his gaze with hot blue eyes that immediately tightened his groin. God almighty, nothing in the world had prepared him for the impact of Josie Reynolds.

Even in prisoner's orange she was not cowed or ashamed. He'd avoided her because he hadn't want to see her hurt. She was down and injured, and he associated that with his mother and the demons he could never slay for her no matter how badly he wanted to. He'd forgotten, however, that Josie was nothing like his mother. Josie came out swinging.

"Stop staring, Stryker," she said. "My hair's not even done."

She turned away haughtily and he wasn't sure whether to applaud or chastise.

"Did you see all the reporters outside of the jail?" she spoke up abruptly, her voice outraged. "Vultures! The whole lot of them are vultures."

"They're the media," Stone said lightly. "It's what they're paid to be."

"Hah! Finnley's brought me the papers. Most of them have drawn and quartered me by now. I think they all need a hobby."

"They have one. You."

Josie scowled. "How long till we get there?"

"Five minutes."

"More press on that end?"

"Of course."

"Vultures. Pure vultures."

The radio crackled to life. Since Jack was driving, Stone picked it up. The dispatcher informed them that there had just been a traffic accident on Main. They would want to take a detour around the outside of town to avoid being caught in the snarl.

Jack nodded and took the right.

"You could stop and assist with the accident," Josie said hopefully from the back. "It's not like I'm in a hurry."

"Transporting prisoners takes precedence," Jack informed her.

"Prisoner," she muttered. "Prisoner. I'm a prisoner. Well, why not? *Honey* and *sweetheart* are so overused."

Jack's hands tightened on the wheel. He could feel Stone's gaze on his cheek but didn't turn. Instead, his eyes went to the rearview mirror, where Josie stared at him with a gaze angry enough to burn down the city.

"I looked into your allegations," he said firmly. "I listened to you that much. Now the matter's out of my hands."

"I have no motive, doubting Thomas. No motive, no motive, no motive."

Jack gave up and stared at the road. Grand Springs was to their left now, a grassy embankment on their right. The road would loop them around the town where they could approach the courthouse from the other side. It would add five minutes to their trip, but that was nothing compared to the time and safety risk a traffic jam posed.

Behind them, a dark sedan approached, otherwise they were alone. Keeping his gaze on the new arrival, Jack slowed for the traffic light. The car slowed as well, breaking behind them with the usual amount of distance. He relaxed a fraction and waited for the light to turn green.

It wasn't until he drove through the light that the sedan sped up. It pulled out as if to pass them, and Jack immediately stepped on the brakes, giving the car every chance to rocket by them. Beside him, Stone was tense, his hand on his holster.

The sedan kept even. Jack hit his brakes, so did the other car.

"Damn," Stone said tightly. He drew out his gun and the dark tinted window slowly rolled down.

There was no time to think. No time to react. No time to feel. Dimly, Jack recognized glowing blond hair. Then abruptly, he caught the strong, overpowering scent: gardenias.

"No!" Josie screamed.

"Down!" Stone yelled.

What's the woman doing with a straw? Jack thought, then felt a sharp prick and reflexively slapped his neck.

Poison dart, he thought as he blacked out at the wheel.

* * *

The car swerved hard. In the back seat, Josie tumbled
to the side. She thought Stone would have a chance to
grab the wheel, but it was already too late. The car plowed
down the embankment, tossing them through the air. She
heard a sickening thud, then a loud crash. Scents of gas
and pine penetrated the car.

The car stopped moving but her head wasn't doing so
well. She shook it twice before the world came into order.

She was flopped across the back seat. In front, Stone
was sprawled over the dashboard, unmoving, and she
could see blood trickling down his forehead.

"Stone? Stone?" He didn't respond and her voice rose
an octave. Her gaze latched onto Jack. He was slumped
over the steering wheel, also unmoving.

"Jack? Jack, can you hear me? Please, Jack?"

He didn't move. She banged on the bulletproof glass
dividing her from the front seat with both hands.

"Dammit, Jack. I take back every evil comment I've
ever made. Now, wake up, okay? Please, please, please,
tell me you're all right."

Jack remained slumped forward. And then she saw the
tiny dart sticking out of the side of his neck.

A poison dart. *A poison dart!* The hysteria bubbled up
in her throat. Of course, a poison dart. Why not a poison
dart? If you're a young, modern woman who suddenly
discovers yourself framed for murder, why shouldn't the
arresting officer be hit by a poison dart?

Holy mother of God, what had happened to her life!
And why? Why, why, why?

"Come on, Stryker. Wake up now. Pull the dart out of
your neck and tell me I'm on 'Candid Camera.' I won't
even hit you for it if you'll just tell me right now."

Tell me you're all right. I need you to be all right.

And then she realized that the dark sedan hadn't driven

away. It was perched on the edge of the road, and even from here, she could see glimpses of blond hair as the driver climbed out.

"Dammit. Think, Josie. And think now!"

She struggled with the back door; of course, it didn't open. Back doors of police cruisers should never yield for prisoners. She banged against the bulletproof glass separating her from the front seat. It didn't even buckle. She was trapped as neatly as a bug in a specimen jar and Jack and Stone were still unmoving.

And then the blonde came fully into focus. She was tall. She was beautiful. She was dressed entirely in a black leotard with a heavy-looking utility belt, as if she'd used Catwoman as a model.

She wasn't carrying a whip, however.

This woman started descending the hillside with one very large gun.

Nine

Josie gave up on fumbling with the back door handle. She kicked out with her feet, hitting the door with as much force as she could muster. The left side didn't budge. Powered by adrenaline and pure desperation, she attacked the right side. It must have already been jarred open by the crash because it burst open immediately. She tumbled out into the grass, glancing over her shoulder.

The blonde was approaching steadily. Her big black gun was already poised.

Josie searched frantically for an escape. If she plunged forward, the ravine eventually opened into a full hillside covered with trees. Perhaps the tall fields of grass would offer her protection.

And Jack and Stone? They were still slumped over in the front seat, unconscious and vulnerable.

The blonde could walk right up to them and end it with two quick pulls of the trigger, just the way it was done in the movies. That quick. That simple.

"Think, Josie, think. Brilliance would be good right about now."

Unfortunately, her brain was taking a momentary vacation to avoid such pleasantries as fear, pain and imminent death.

She settled for moving. She raced around the back of the car and opened Jack's door in one smooth swoop, ducking behind the door for cover. The approaching woman looked right at her, her expression cool and remote.

She didn't say anything, she didn't pause. She just kept descending, slow and steady.

And Josie understood that the woman also knew her targets were immobile—she knew she had plenty of time.

Josie yanked the dart out of Jack's neck, gripped his shoulders, and shook him hard.

"Come on, Jack. Wake up for me."

Jack moaned, his eyes still closed. The blonde appeared just twenty feet away. Now she stopped. Now she leveled her strange, long-barreled gun.

Josie's brain finally fired to life. She grabbed for Jack's revolver.

"No, dammit," he groaned. His fingers wrapped reflexively around her wrist, trying to protect his gun. They wrestled for the weapon like children while the neighborhood assassin took aim.

"I'm trying to save your miserable hide!" Josie muttered through gritted teeth. "Now, give it here!"

His fingers abruptly loosened. She pulled the gun out of the holster triumphantly, already fumbling with the safety thing and thinking that the gun was much too big and much too loud and she was going to get them all killed.

The handcuff slapped around her left wrist abruptly. The following click brought her gaze to Jack's right wrist, where he'd just joined them in unholy matrimony. Even as she watched, he tossed the key out into the deep grass.

"Kill me and you're trapped," he murmured thickly. His blue eyes, heavy-lidded and glazed, still held a determined gleam.

"You stupid fool—oh, my God!"

A whistling sound emitted. Josie ducked and something whizzed by her ear. She stared up an inch to see a needle sticking out of the rubber molding around the window. The woman had opened fire with a tranquilizer gun. And Josie was willing to bet those needles contained something a little more potent than the one she'd pulled out of Jack's neck. Perhaps one hundred percent pure potassium or something even worse.

She turned, shut her eyes and opened fire. Then she remembered she was supposed to look at her target, so she opened her eyes and squeezed back the trigger a few more times. The woman dove for cover in the thick grass. Jack groaned and winced as if she'd hit him. Maybe in his drugged world she had.

Josie didn't waste time. She had absolutely no experience with guns, but the damn thing seemed big enough and it made a lot of noise. She fired into the grass twice more and was rewarded by the black shape slithering to the side. She fired a third time and a cloud of dirt plumed up.

"Get out of here," Josie cried out at the top of her lungs. "Get back into your car or I'll blow your brains out."

The blonde didn't move, however. After a moment, Josie realized that she couldn't. Heading up the hillside would expose her immediately to gunfire, so she had no choice but to lie low and use the grass for cover. Josie had actually pinned her in.

She'd trapped them all.

She caught a glimmer of blond movement and fired. The woman bobbed back down. Josie sat there, her hand beginning to shake. How many bullets did she have? She had no idea. And what would she do once she ran out?

Jack was slumped back against the seat, his eyes open, and he was shaking his head as if trying to ward off a bad dream. Stone finally groaned, beginning to come around.

Josie made her decision. She slapped Jack hard.

"Wake up, Stryker. Time to make the doughnuts. One, two, three!"

She yanked on her handcuffed wrist as hard as possible,

tumbling both of them into the grass. The blond woman bobbed up immediately and Josie scrambled to open fire.

"No," Jack cried hoarsely.

"Yes!" Josie cried back vehemently. "Now run, dammit, run!"

She staggered to her feet, her butt in the air, and dragged him forward. He protested, but when the blonde reappeared and Josie fired again, he suddenly rocketed forward as if she were shooting at him. Whatever worked.

Behind them she heard a whistle and dropped immediately. Ahead of her, a bush shuddered as the dart hit.

"Jack, move!"

She lunged forward, dragging him the best she could. They'd made it only three feet when she heard another whistle and yanked them down. Jack fell better than he walked. His skin had taken on a horrible pallor. Sweat burst out of his pores.

And another dart whistled by.

They were going to die, Josie thought. They were really going to die. Jack was poisoned and hurt. She was chained and inexperienced. Stan Reynolds's street-smart daughter had finally met her match. She didn't even understand what was going on, or who would try to do this to her.

The grass to her right rippled. She caught a glimpse of blond hair and fired.

Jack moaned and muttered on the ground. His body jerked convulsively.

Josie took his hand, wincing at the clammy, cold feel of his skin.

"It'll be all right," she murmured desperately. "It'll be all right, Stryker. I'll take care of you."

I won't let you die.

The grass rippled. She raised her gun and fired.

And the trigger pulled back with an empty click.

Empty. Empty!

The blonde rose up smoothly. There was no expression on her face. She did not look triumphant or gleeful. In that instant of time, Josie met her gaze and knew she'd never met this woman. They were not enemies, they were not old acquaintances.

The woman would kill her, but it was nothing personal.

The woman leveled her strange gun smoothly. She aimed it at Josie's heart.

And gunfire rocketed the air. Josie flinched, but the blond woman spun around, taking aim behind her and firing as she fell into the grass. Josie saw Stone with his gun, then abruptly he was diving for cover, as well.

She didn't wait. She tugged Jack's hand and whispered with all her heart, "Run, Jack Stryker. And do it now!"

He lurched up drunkenly and they staggered forward.

Josie didn't have a plan. She pulled Jack the best she could into the thick cover of forest, the empty gun tucked in her waistband because maybe Jack would have extra ammunition on him, and, most likely, they would need the gun again.

She was a city girl at heart. She didn't know about tracking, but she was pretty sure a two-year-old could follow their trail at this point. She'd once read that you should drag tree branches after you to cover footprints. Somehow, that seemed to be an odd thing to do when Catwoman could appear anytime with her poisoned darts.

Josie resorted to speed. She dragged Jack down the brush-covered hillside with branches and brambles tearing at her cheeks. Thrashing to the bottom, they came to a road. On the other side, the true forest began. Josie raced right toward it.

Jack made it across, then tripped over a small rock and fell hard, taking her with him. The air left her with a rush. She staggered up, anyway, then her legs gave out and she crumpled back down. Her chest was on fire. Sweat mixed with mud and thorns and blood on her cheeks. Her hands burned from a hundred small cuts.

But she was too terrified to stop. The blonde would come. The blonde would kill them.

Josie had seen it in her eyes.

"Come on, Jack," she whispered hoarsely. "Come on."

He didn't moan, he didn't speak. His face had gone from pallor to flush, and a lean, haggard look hollowed out his cheeks. His body was trembling, his hand clutched his knee.

She was stunned by shadows deepening around his eyes. He looked like a man on a death march.

"Jack?" She couldn't keep the fear out of her voice.

His lips moved. They were parched and cracked, and it took a moment for the word to escape.

He said, "Move."

She did.

She didn't know how long they ran this time. It seemed like forever, but given their condition, she doubted it was that long. Her arm and shoulder ached from pulling Jack along. Her cheeks and hands stung from all the scrapes. Her muscles were liquefying.

Jack stumbled a lot. They would stagger up and keep going. But each time, it took them longer and longer to get to their feet. The sixth time, Josie just couldn't do it. She rolled toward him, lying on her back and struggling for big, deep gulps of air. Beside her, Jack's shoulders trembled horribly.

"Can you sit up?" she asked at last.

"M-m-maybe." It took him three attempts to finally flop against a tree trunk. He looked exhausted.

"De…hydrated," he whispered.

"Oh." Of course, the man had sweat bullets, then run

through half the state. He probably required a gallon or two. Her eyes filled up.

"I don't have water," she said soggily. "I...I don't have anything."

"Stream."

"Where? Just tell me where, I'll get you water."

"Can't. Handcuffs." He raised his cuffed hand wearily. Now she was sure she was going to cry. The tension and fear were catching up with her and she was just a little bit hysterical.

She squeezed her eyes shut.

"Jack," she said after a moment, her voice steadier. "We have to move again. Do you know how to find the stream?"

He nodded slowly.

"All right. I'll stand first, then help you up. We can take it slower, but we have to get there." She glanced over her shoulder. So far, there was no sign of pursuit. Maybe Stone had shot the blond woman.

Or maybe she'd shot Stone.

She focused on Jack, not wanting to contemplate the rest. "Ready?"

His hand formed a weak thumbs-up. She climbed to her feet. It took them two tries to get Jack up, but once standing he could walk. She put her shoulder beneath his, helping him the best she could and trying to hold back the worst of the tree branches before they lost the last of their skin.

They plunged deeper into the woods. The trees choked out the sunlight. The air took on the rich, musty scent of drying leaves that never saw the light of day. The temperature dropped, and Josie began to shake as much as Jack.

She didn't know where they were. The towering trees thwarted her sense of direction. Scurrying noises and small scuffles made her wonder what kind of companions the forest would bring. She followed Jack gamely, willing him not to pass out, because if he did, they would both succumb to dehydration and exposure, chained together like escaped felons. When Josie had been a little girl, she'd dreamed of meeting a big handsome man just like her father, and loving him the way her mother loved Stan. Somehow, in all those girlish fantasies, she'd never gotten around to dying handcuffed to a stubborn cop on a lonely mountainside.

It made her want to laugh hysterically or maybe weep. It was hard to decide.

They walked grimly, Jack's fingers woven into hers, and Josie held on tight.

Eventually, she heard a new sound. Water gurgling over stones. Jack took them straight to the side of the stream.

They both stared at the clear, flowing water. So beautiful, so cold, so beguiling. Neither of them moved.

"Pollution," Josie whispered. "Runoff from the old mines and farming. Do you think it's safe?"

"I don't know."

"I've read that hikers often do themselves in by drinking contaminated water."

"I know."

"Jack...I'm scared."

His fingers tightened around hers. He lifted his other hand tiredly and smoothed back her brambled hair. His gaze searched hers, no promises, no lies. Handcuffed together on the mountainside, running from someone they didn't even know, they'd finally found common ground. "I'm scared, too," he whispered hoarsely.

He got down on his stomach and began to scoop the water into his mouth with his free hand. After a moment, she followed.

* * *

Half an hour later, they leaned back against an outcropping of rocks and tried to pull themselves together.

"How do you feel?" she asked at last.

"Like hell."

"That good?" His coloring had improved, at least. His breathing was also easier. She could see a small red bump alongside his neck, almost like a mosquito bite. Was that how it was supposed to look, like Jack had just lost control of the vehicle, killing them all? And the blonde had followed up with her poison gun just to be sure?

Josie didn't want to contemplate such things, but she figured she'd better.

Jack rubbed his temples. "The blonde" he murmured at last. "She hit me with quite a round of something."

"Ding, ding, ding. The man wins a prize."

"Do you know who she is?"

"I don't have any idea. I think…I think she's an assassin of some type. She's very professional, Jack. And very…very cold."

"You took my gun." His voice was still thick, his forehead crinkling as he struggled to piece together hazy images. "Do you still have it?"

"Yes." She pulled it out from her waistband. "I used up all the bullets, though. Do you have more?"

He frowned, not seeming to have heard her question. "Stone?"

She hesitated. "I don't know. He regained consciousness. He fired at her, too. I'm not sure what happened after that."

"We should go back," he said immediately.

Josie took a deep breath. "No."

"Stone—"

"—knows how to take care of himself. Besides, at this

point, what could we do for him, Jack? Whatever has happened, has happened.''

Jack shook his head. ''We have no food…we have no supplies…we both look like hell.''

''Look, I know it's hard to think clearly when you're pumped full of God knows what, but just hear me out for a minute. I did not kill Olivia. I'm not a cop, but I would say Catwoman's affinity for poison darts and the scent of gardenias moves her to the number-one-suspect box. Plus, there's the matter that she tried to kill us.''

''But—''

Josie held up her hand. ''I'm not done yet. So let's say Catwoman is the real killer. Who is she? I don't know her, you don't know her. She was too serious, too cold to be doing this for personal reasons. I think she was hired.''

Slowly, Jack nodded. Encouraged, Josie continued, ''So someone paid her. We don't know who or why. But we do know they went to some pretty great lengths to frame me for the crime, then tried to kill me before the case went to trial, probably thinking my death would close things out. Jack…that person had to have a lot of inside information and, well, power.''

Jack was back to frowning. She took a deep breath and covered his hand with hers. She knew he wouldn't like what she was about to say. ''We left for the courthouse, they had to know about that.''

''Everyone knew.''

''The dark sedan just happened to find us on the detour?''

''The accident on Main,'' he argued sluggishly. ''You're…saying they caused an *accident* on Main just…so we'd…drive around? No. Too far…fetched.''

''What if there wasn't an accident on Main? What if that was just a message to get us on the side route where there was amazingly little traffic considering all the other

gaze how much he cared for her, how well he knew her, and how vehemently he swore never to doubt her again.

His mouth closed over her breast. His tongue rolled over her nipple. She gripped his head tighter against her and begged him thickly never to stop.

Together they fumbled with her jumpsuit, finally getting it wadded on the chain between them. The uniform panties disappeared quickly, her fingers moving faster than his.

And then for one moment they stopped. Josie looked at him. She could hear her own loud breathing in the silence. She could hear his shallow gasps, as well. His blue eyes were clear, deep and wanting. She could feel his intensity and desire across the small space separating their naked bodies. She saw his honest need.

"I love you," she said without preamble.

He faltered visibly, looking stunned. "It's the situation—"

"No, Stryker, it's love. That thing everyone else has always known about but me."

"But I doubted you. I arrested you—"

"You did your job, just the way you promised."

"Josie…"

His words trailed off. He grimaced. She felt a thin thread of fear, but it stiffened her conviction. She hadn't made the declaration because she'd wanted something in return. She'd told him because she meant it and she felt he had the right to know. Her parents hadn't been perfect, but they'd taught her many things—love was to be shared, openly, honestly and generously.

And being here with Jack, feeling everything blooming in her chest, she understood why her father took the sales jobs he hated for her mother. And she understood why her mother forgave him when he got back into the game. And she understood why they raised her with so many smiles and fresh-baked cookies in a kitchen that smelled of nutmeg and vanilla.

Someday, she wanted to have a little girl—or maybe a little boy—and then she would share with them all the beautiful moments her parents had shared with her.

''Kiss me, Stryker. Hold me. Make love to me. Later, we'll talk about 'one step at a time.'''

She pressed herself against him, and the first tantalizing touch of bare skin against bare skin made them both catch their breaths.

''You're beautiful,'' he whispered thickly, his mouth against her neck. ''You're amazing.''

And then his mouth was once more on her breast and she wasn't thinking or talking and he wasn't thinking or talking. She was feeling every touch he made, arching her body toward him, wrapping her fingers around him and urging him even closer.

Her legs parted. She guided him between her thighs, knowing already what she wanted. Her hips arched up. He rubbed against her and she bit her lip with the intensity.

Then suddenly, he was pulling back.

''Josie, I still don't have protection.''

''I know.''

''We shouldn't—''

She opened her eyes. She looked at him clearly. ''No, Jack. We should. This is exactly what we should do.''

And then he was lost and they both knew it. His lips were on hers earnestly, his hands stroking her hair. His touch was gentle, his touch was tender. He told her everything she needed to know, everything he still couldn't quite put into words.

She guided him to her body and arched back her neck and gave herself over to wonder.

The first penetration was slow. It had been a long time for her, a long time for him. There was a moment of un-

believable beauty when she opened her eyes again and
thought, this is Jack Stryker, inside my body, moving in
me, joining with me.

Then it felt too good to think. She closed her eyes. She
gripped his flanks and urged him faster, finding his rhythm,
hearing his harsh breath, knowing that it was right.

"Josie," he gasped. His body thrust hard. "I love you,
too."

And then she was crying his name and they were tumbling over the abyss and she tasted sweat on her lips and
held him even closer.

"I love you, Jack. I love you."

"I'm going to get into the lake now."

"Sorry, Stryker, but I'm too sore to have sex again so
soon."

He rolled his eyes. "No, I mean I'm honestly going to
get into the lake now." Then abruptly, his face scrunched
up with concern. He brushed back her hair. "Did I hurt
you?"

"Horribly. Wanna do it again tonight?" She smiled at
him eagerly and he shook his head.

"You're incorrigible."

She ran her finger down his naked, muscled arm. "And
you're really sexy for a man who's run up a mountain and
crawled through a cave. Tell me, do you handcuff all your
women?"

"Just the ones I don't want to get away."

"Oh, Stryker, that's good. I didn't realize you could be
so smooth."

"Hah." He actually appeared indignant. "I have lots of
talents you don't know about yet, since you seem to enjoy
sparking my temper first and forgoing the rest. I happen
to be very charming."

"Of course."

"I also have good taste in wine, restaurants and jewelry."

"Wow, I chose better than I thought. What else?"

"Let's see… Christmas presents should only be opened Christmas morning—"

"Spoilsport."

"Children should always be read bedtime stories, couples should always walk hand in hand, and husbands should be served breakfast in bed on Sundays. I like my eggs over easy."

"Oh, I bet you do," she said, but she was smiling too broadly to sound firm. "I'll agree to bedtime stories and walking hand in hand. The rest we'll have to discuss."

"Okay. You open your presents Christmas Eve, then serve me breakfast in bed. Compromise is so easy."

She shook her head, tried to push him playfully, then got sidetracked kissing him again. It was warm and wonderful, and yet when they pulled away, neither could escape the chill.

The cavern with still gray with daylight. They could see better. So could their pursuer.

"Stone," Jack murmured after a while. His face was already somber.

"I'm sure he's okay."

"No, you're not. Neither of us is." He lapsed into taut silence.

After a moment, Josie briskly rubbed his arm. "All right, let's both get into the lake and clean up. Then we'll move on. You said there's an exit tunnel?"

Jack nodded, still distracted by thoughts of his partner, and pointed up. Josie stared obligingly at the ceiling, but didn't see any signs marked Exit.

"Where?"

"Up there." He jerked his head. "See that hole? You go out through there."

"Uh, Jack. That's thirty feet in the air."

"Yeah." He gave her a rueful smile and shrugged. "We're not exactly on a vacation here, Josie. We're trying to escape from an experienced assassin, and, well, that involves doing a few things I'm sure accountants don't normally do. Honestly, a beginner can do this climb. Once we go over to the wall, you'll see that there are plenty of places for your feet and hands. I'll go first, finding all the handholds, and you can follow me. We've made it this far. We'll be okay."

Josie looked at the yawning well and the opening so far above them. She looked at Jack. He was right. They were in a tough spot and they would do what they had to do.

"Okay, let's bathe quickly."

Jack climbed into the water first, not jumping since that would drag her in. He shivered a bit, but indicated it wasn't bad, so she gingerly stuck her foot in. It didn't feel slimy or salty. It was just…well, water.

She gave up and climbed in. The hundreds of scratches on her arms and legs flared to life and she sucked in her breath. Beside her, Jack laughed tightly.

"Feels great, doesn't it?"

"How can you stand it?" She'd seen his legs. He ought to be dancing a jig by now.

"I'm a man, I'm tough," he said in a deep baritone. Then he murmured in his real voice, "Besides, my arms hurt too much to pull me back out."

Josie laughed, and for a moment, they both felt better. They scrubbed each other's backs the best they could and went to work on their faces. If they stayed close to the edge, they could stand on a rock shelf; otherwise it got too deep and they had to tread water. With a ton of soaked clothes hanging between them, that was hard to do.

Finally, they both sat on the stone rim, and scrubbed

their clothes the best they could. They got so into the task, they didn't hear any noise behind them.

Jack had just pulled on his underwear when Josie caught a movement out of the corner of her eye. Strange that a shadow should be moving.

Then she froze, and then she knew.

She heard the high-pitched whistle first. She grabbed Jack's shoulder without thinking and shouted "Down!" at the top of her lungs.

They fell into the water face first. Josie felt the chain between them go tight as Jack dove deeper than she did. For one moment, she jerked back hard, panicked by the feeling of being dragged down. He countered, and they both shot to the top, sputtering and dazed.

The woman in black stood on the shore. Her black leotard was now torn from her own journey through the tunnel, and her hair was a tangled blond mess. None of it seemed to affect her.

She looked at them squarely, raised her dart gun and wordlessly fired again.

They split, diving to the side to avoid the dart. Instantly, Josie realized the woman's strategy. She wasn't trying to get both of them, she was just trying to get one. One drugged person, sinking to the bottom of the lake and taking her handcuffed partner with her to a watery grave.

Did you ever wonder how the people on the Titanic *felt?*

Josie fought her way to the surface desperately. Her lungs burned, her limbs thrashed with panic. She saw the woman, already taking aim. She heard Jack, yelling in her ear.

"Inhale now!"

The whistle split the air. A dart fired through the shadows. Josie gasped, Josie inhaled, and then abruptly she was jerked down into the lake, Jack diving beneath the surface and dragging her with him. Down, down, down they went.

Nothing to see, nothing to hear. Once more, the unbearable blackness pressed against her.

Still Jack went down.

Falling, falling, falling.

And then Josie realized that the woman had finally hit her mark.

Twelve

She couldn't see, she couldn't hear. The claustrophobia was worse than even the tunnel; she could feel the thick black water pressing against her eardrums, thrusting into the tender membranes of her nose, lips and gums. The water was clutching at her, tearing at her, fighting to get inside her where it would own her completely.

And still she sank down, down, down, Jack's heavy body too much for her to counteract.

Josie, Josie, do something!

She tried to twist her body, but Jack's deadweight wouldn't let her. She tried to kick her feet, but it had no effect whatsoever. Her lungs burned. A dull roar built inside her head. Her eardrums were going to burst.

Something slimy and small brushed against her leg. She kicked out reflexively, gave in to panic and struggled in earnest.

Abruptly, Jack's fingers curled around her handcuffed wrist. He angled straight and Josie felt his legs begin to kick. He was swimming, he was leading. He wasn't unconscious or dead, after all. He was following a plan. She struggled behind him, trying to make her legs work when her throat was gasping for oxygen, tickling her gag reflex. At any moment, she wasn't sure she'd be able to control it. She would choke, and the silty water would rush into her lungs.

Her hand hit slimy surface and recoiled to her side. Jack tugged her forward. Belatedly, she realized she'd hit a wall. They'd arrived at the perimeter of the cavern. Jack's legs were still kicking and churning.

Her legs struggled with their own little kicks, no more than little flutters. But then she realized the water was no longer so black. She saw a steady lightening. They were in a tunnel, and ahead, there was light!

She joined Jack swimming in earnest. Her lungs hurt, her ears hurt. Her head throbbed unbearably. So much pressure. She wanted to breathe. She needed to breathe. She was desperate to breathe.

With one last fierce kick, Jack rocketed them out of the tunnel and toward the light. Up, up, up. The rapid ascent expanded her blood vessels until she thought her eyes would burst from her skull. Faster, faster, faster.

They broke free, their heads firing above the surface, their mouths opening and gulping for air like leaping bass. Her ears popped. She crashed back into the water, treading frantically to keep her head up and the oxygen flowing. Josie had never been in so much pain. And she had never felt so glorious. They were back in the great outdoors, the daytime sky huge and vast above them.

She was never going to live indoors again. After this damn thing, she was going to sleep outdoors surrounded by oxygen and sunlight for the rest of her life!

Her muscles abruptly gave up and she almost sunk beneath the water, except Jack pulled her back up.

"The shore," Jack gasped weakly.

She followed. They had to rest their heads against the bank for a full minute before they could contemplate pulling themselves out.

"I'll go first," Jack said at last. "Help you out."

"The…woman?"

"Still in cavern. Probably thinks we're dead. Hope… so."

"Me…too."

Jack pulled himself up on arms that trembled like spaghetti and beached himself on the dirt edge with all the grace of a whale. He pulled Josie's arm up with him, but she was too tired to follow. Her other hand was wrapped around some reeds, and she clung to them as if they would keep her afloat.

"Come on," Jack said at last.

She groaned. Their clothes were soaked and tangled between them on the handcuffs. Jack, when he stood, was naked except for his underwear. She tried to stir the interest and energy such a sight merited, but she was beyond even that at the moment. She wanted a hot shower. Robbed of adrenaline and starved of rest, her body was now collapsing.

"On the count of three," Jack murmured. He hunkered down and offered her his hand. His blond hair was plastered against his skull. His face was finally free of mud and twigs after their swim. Now she could see his true pallor. And she could see the goose bumps shivering his skin as the cool morning air slapped against his water-soaked form.

"Did she hit you again?" Josie asked immediately, searching for signs of a feathered dart. "I thought she did."

Jack frowned and shook his head. "Not me, you?"

"Not me."

"All right, then." Jack counted to three, then lunged back, popping Josie out of the water. She beached with about the same elegance he had. And the cool morning air hit her just as fiercely.

"Sweet mother of God," she whispered through clenched teeth. Abruptly, she couldn't stop shivering.

"Put on your suit." Jack ordered crisply. He was already moving, struggling to untangle his ruined dress shirt.

"We can't wander around like this. We're too close to exposure."

The urgency of his tone infected her actions. She jumped to, though her thick, trembling fingers took forever to do such simple tasks as smooth out pant legs and fasten snaps. After a few misdirections, she managed to get her jumpsuit on. The cold, wet material stuck to her like a second skin and sent more chills up her spine.

"I've never been so cold for so long," she whispered through chattering teeth.

Jack just nodded. She could see that his fingers were turning blue. He couldn't get his shirt to button.

"Here let me."

"No, I got it."

"Dammit, Jack, let me!" Her fierce tone stopped him. She seized the opportunity to button the soggy material all the way to his neck, then began to briskly rub his arms. The shirttails hung to the top of his thighs, but his legs were bare, wheat blond hair standing up like a hissing cat's. Under any other circumstances, he would've looked comic. Now, his half-dressed, half-drowned state filled her with panic. He was dangerously close to succumbing to exposure.

"You're not going to give up on me, Jack Stryker," she whispered fiercely.

"I would never do such a thing to a lady," he promised and held her hand.

They made it to the mountain road. They flagged down Mr. Chouder in his beat-up pickup truck, who was too polite to ask about Jack's missing pants and too smart to question why they were handcuffed together. From the old school, he blasted the truck's decrepit heater and talked politely of the weather as he drove. Jack directed him to Stone and Jessica's house. He wanted to know if his partner was okay. And it was probably the only location where he knew they would be safe. Twenty-four hours after their ordeal had begun, Jack and Josie still didn't know who was behind the mysterious blonde, nor why. They needed rest. They needed food. They needed answers.

Mr. Chouder finally pulled up to the house. He merely said, "You take care of yourself, Miss Reynolds." He eyed Jack meaningfully.

"I understand, sir," Jack said, trying to appear dignified and somber as he stood on the roadside in his white B.V.D.s and buttoned-up dress shirt.

Mr. Chouder looked at him one last time, openly skeptical, then finally drove away.

Josie began to giggle. The traitorous laughter started in her belly and bubbled out of her throat. She was pretty sure she'd lost it. Jack was rapping firmly on the door, half-naked and scowling with wounded dignity.

By the time Jessica answered the door, Josie was giggling so hard she couldn't talk. She looked at Jessica's widening eyes. She looked at Jack, standing with his arms on his hips as if he showed up every day in just his underwear, and she laughed so hard she had to sit down on the porch, rocking back and forth.

In the distance, she heard Jessica speaking to Jack. Stone was at the police station. Stone was all right. Stone had been looking for them both all night.

And then Jessica's gaze was on her, but Josie couldn't stop laughing and rocking back and forth.

"It's all right now," Jessica said softly. "You'll be fine here. You'll be safe."

Then Jack's arm was curling around her shoulders and she stopped laughing and began to cry.

An hour later, freshly showered and weighed down by warm clothes, Josie and Jack sat at the kitchen table,

spooning hot chicken noodle soup into their mouths with
the restraint of four-year-olds.

"Cwwakrs," Josie mumbled with her mouth full, hand
thrust out for the crackers. Jessica obediently slapped a roll
of saltines into her palm.

"Chwwse," Jack demanded through a mouthful of
crackers. Jessica sliced a quarter of a brick more. Josie and
Jack fell on the slices like cave people who'd starved all
winter. Beyond dignity, they both swiped at the last piece,
grappled for it fiercely, then lost it to Jessica, who was still
moving faster than they were. She diplomatically cut it into
two pieces, handing them each half before they inflicted
bodily harm. She was still surprised they hadn't choked to
death on the crackers. At this point, it appeared they were
forgoing such social graces as chewing.

Of course, it wasn't every day a woman had a young
couple sitting handcuffed at her kitchen table. Jack had
managed to break the chain linking the metal bracelets
using the wire cutters from Stone's tool kit, but he hadn't
been able to open the bracelets decorating each of their
wrists. At least breaking the chain permitted them to finally
strip off their soaked clothes and don new ones. Josie was
wearing Jessica's turtleneck, sweater and jeans. She also
had a blanket on her lap. Jack was wearing Stone's turtleneck sweater, a pair of sweatpants and two pairs of thick
wool hiking socks. The color was finally returning to his
cheeks.

They had just begun scraping the bottom of their bowls
when Stone finally burst through the front door.

Three pairs of eyes met him instantly. Jessica's gaze
softened instinctively, her nerves tingling a bit as they always did when she saw her husband. Jack's face brightened with immediate relief, his muscles finally relaxing
when he saw that his partner was indeed safe. Josie's ears

picked up, her gaze earnestly searching the newcomer for signs of grocery bags. She was still hungry.

"Thank God," Stone said at last, speaking for everyone in the kitchen.

Josie gave up on him; he obviously hadn't stopped at the grocery store on the way home from the police station. "More soup?" She held out her bowl hopefully, dragging her handcuff into sight.

Jessica sighed and rose to search her cupboards, which were rapidly being depleted. Stone gazed at the handcuff on Josie's wrist in shock. "What the hell...?"

"Stryker did it," Josie said promptly, sitting back when it became apparent more food was on the way. "He got it into his drugged skull that I was trying to kill him, so he handcuffed me to him."

She looked down at their wrists and abruptly scowled. Finally washed, clothed and fed, she had time to truly contemplate the damage. Her wrist sported dark purple bruises and deeply cut rings. Some of the cuts had begun to bleed around the edges from her fresh burst of movement.

"We should get the cuffs off," Jack said softly. "We probably both need to get our wrists wrapped."

Stone was already moving. He took a key out of his pocket and in one deft movement released both cuffs. Josie's metal bracelet fell dully on the kitchen table. Her arm rose a notch before she caught it, feeling weightless now that it had been freed. She looked at Jack and saw that he felt as strange as she did. An odd awkwardness abruptly fell between them. The handcuffs had joined them for the last twenty-four hours. Now the last vestige of their union was gone. They were no longer a team. They sat at the kitchen table as two free individuals.

Jack cleared his throat. He looked down at his empty soup bowl.

Jessica retrieved a first aid kit and got them through the

next few moments by passing out antiseptic and bandages. Josie picked up the yellow tube of healing ointment, not sure what to do.

"Let me," Jack said. He cradled her forearm gently in his hand and his touch was light, soothing. It was all right, he told her with his hand. They were all right. *One step at a time.*

"I looked for you all night," Stone said abruptly. "We've had dogs out, the volunteer firefighters. God, Jack, where have you been?"

"Underground." Briefly, Jack recapped events. "And you? How did you get away?"

Stone grimaced. "I didn't. She grazed me with one of her darts and I went nighty-night. When I came to, she was gone, you were gone. Hell, there was just me and the squad car and one helluva headache. I radioed for backup immediately, but you guys must have had a solid head start. I can tell you one thing. That woman knows how to cover her tracks."

"She's gotta be a professional," Jack stated. "The way she moved, the way she was armed. Someone hired her, Stone. Someone paid her to hit Olivia, then paid her more to frame Josie for the crime. It was someone high up, Stone. Someone who could plant stories of false detours on police radios."

Stone frowned. Like any good cop, he didn't like conspiracy theories or exotic assassins. Police work was about facts and statistics, not folklore. The numbers said the majority of murders were committed by someone the victim knew. So if you think the estranged husband did it, he probably did. If you think the mayor's friend did it because she was angling for the mayor's job, you were probably right. But Stone had seen the blond hit woman for himself. Moreover, he'd caught the scent of gardenias that surrounded her like a cloud.

"Think about it," Jack said. "Those first darts she fired weren't fatal, they just knocked a person out. So I fall unconscious, drive us off the road. Best case scenario is that Josie dies in the accident and the case is closed. We think Olivia's killer is dead and no one is the wiser."

"But who?" Stone persisted, still shaking his head.

"That's what we have to figure out. Somebody with money, somebody with power. Maybe the person was hired by the infiltrating drug gangs. Maybe one of the CEOs of the strip mining companies has particularly aggressive business practices. Maybe it is personal. You know, there's a lot about Olivia we just don't know." He hesitated, glancing at Josie.

She shrugged. "She didn't tell me anything, Stryker. Like I said, we respected each other's privacy. My impression was that her first marriage was unhappy, her husband's death not completely a bad thing. But she struggled a lot back then. Her oldest son ran away. She was a strong woman, a smart woman, a generous woman. But yes, I think she had a lot of regrets."

Jack frowned and rubbed his temples. "In other words, we're back at the beginning. Well, someone hired Blondie, because she sure as hell isn't doing this for the cheap thrills." He pinned his gaze on Stone. "You didn't tell anyone I was here, right?"

"Sure, Jack, I broadcasted it through the whole town. I followed your directions. I told people I was meeting my lovely wife for lunch and here I am. Just in time to rescue her from your insatiable appetites, I see."

"They've reduced the kitchen to bones," Jessica agreed.

"We should leave," Jack said abruptly. Josie looked at him with mild surprise, as did Stone. Jack's face had taken on that tight look she knew too well.

"Jack—"

"No, listen to me. We didn't die in the car accident. We survived and we saw her. She'll come looking for us."

"She thinks we're dead," Josie protested.

"Not for long. She's a professional, she's thorough. We saw that for ourselves. I don't think she'll assume anything until she's attended our funeral. I bet after a bit, she dove for our bodies. Maybe she even went back and got gear for it. She won't just walk away, Josie. You know it, too."

Josie sagged in her chair. She remembered the cold, expressionless look on the woman's face and she knew Jack was right. The woman wasn't like a mere mortal. More like a robot, programmed to kill and relentless until that mission was accomplished. Slowly, she raised her gaze and looked at Stone.

"You saw her, too," she said quietly.

Stone stilled. In the silence, Jessica sucked in her breath as her gaze focused on her husband.

"You should go away," Jack said immediately. "Take that honeymoon you've always promised Jessica. Just get out of Grand Springs."

"No. I should go with you."

"And Jessica? Who will watch her, Stone? Who will look out for her?"

Stone's gaze fell on his new wife. They had faced danger together before, but that was when Stone had been held hostage by a bank robber. Then the threat had been against him. He had known how scared Jessica had been, but he'd never truly understood it until this moment, when he looked at her and realized his job had just put her in danger.

"Go away," Jack suggested softly. "Take Jessica out of town. I still have the advantage. No one knows where I am or even if I am really alive. I'll find her, Stone. I'll fix it."

Josie's lips thinned. "We'll find her."

"Now, Josie..." he began soothingly.

She cut him off by slamming her fist against the table-top. Jessica and Stone both flinched. "Don't 'now, Josie' me, Jack Stryker! You're doing what you always do and you know it—you're taking the whole world on your shoulders. Well, you can't fix this one alone. This kind of affects me, too. There's the minor detail that my best friend was killed by this woman. Then I lost my reputation and career to her. Oh, yes, and in the last twenty-four hours I almost lost my life. Well that's it!" Her voice rose a fierce octave. "I'm not losing anything else to Super Chick, and that includes you!"

Josie glared at him with all the force and fury she could muster. At the other end of the table, Jessica began politely clapping.

"That was super," she said. "You two are perfect for each other."

Josie didn't take her gaze off Jack, though. She meant what she said. They had been partners for the last twenty-four hours because of the handcuffs, and it had worked. She didn't want to give that up because the metal bracelets were gone. She loved this man. Love meant teamwork. Love meant sharing. Love meant allowing the person to help you.

Jack, however, looked away. Straight Arrow Stryker, still standing alone.

Josie's eyes began to burn.

"Look," Stone said after a moment, breaking the awkward silence, "there's a lot to wade through here and most of us have been up all night. It's almost afternoon, both of you need sleep. Stay until tomorrow morning. Jessica and I will man the fort while you rest. I'll talk to the chief—"

"Don't tell him where we are—"

"I won't tell him, Jack. Give me some credit. But...

Your mom's not doing too well, Jack," Stone said quietly. "You know how she is. Basically, you're listed MIA. She's…she's upset."

Jack closed his eyes. The tension was etched painfully into his haggard face. "I'll call her—"

"Enough," Josie said. She stood abruptly and took his hand. "We have been on the run all night and have come within an inch of being killed. You need sleep, Jack, and rest. Stone will call your mother. Stone and Jessica will stand guard. *I* am taking you to bed." She threaded her fingers through his. "Trust the people you love," she said quietly. "Believe in us, Jack, the way we believe in you." She drew him out of his chair gently. His face was abruptly haggard. He looked at Stone.

"We're fine," Stone reiterated. "We have an APB out on the blond woman, and I'm going to ask for extra patrols around the house. I've been in tight spots before, Jack, and been all right. Now, you listen to Josie. She's got a good head on her shoulders."

Josie took that as a dismissal and led Jack down the hall. The news about his mother seemed to have taken the last reserves from him. He didn't protest as she led him into the guest room. He stood silently in the middle while she closed the door, then lowered the blinds and cast the room into shadows.

"Josie," he said after a moment. "Thank you." She stripped off his clothes and tucked him into bed. A moment later, after casting off her own clothes, she joined him between the sheets.

As always, she was amazed by the feel of his bare skin against hers. She was enthralled by the heat of his skin, the smooth, delicate texture of his back. She curled up around him spoon-style. She stroked his hair, then his cheek, then his arm, until she felt the last of the tension drain out of him. He brushed her hand. He turned, and threaded his fingers slowly through her hair.

"I love you, Jack Stryker," she said.

There was a ponderous moment when she felt his gaze glitter in the dark. Then his lips brushed hers, again, again and again. Until suddenly he was fierce and he was needy and he held her like a drowning man, letting her see his vulnerability, letting her share his load. They lay tangled together for a long, long time, savoring the embrace. Josie's eyes began to drift shut. Right before she fell asleep, she heard Jack whisper, "I love you, too, Josie." And everything was all right. They slept tightly intertwined, not letting each other go.

She dove down once, twice, then three times. She combed the endless bottom of the silty darkness until her lungs burned painfully and her leg muscles hurt as she kicked. She felt around with her hands, trusting them to guide her as they had so many times before.

Patiently, resiliently, she dove and searched, dove and searched.

The third time, instead of finding two clasped bodies, she found the tunnel, and Joanna Jackson knew her quarry had escaped. She surfaced once, took another deep gulp of air, and then as naturally as a seal or otter, dove back into the oily blackness, rocketing gracefully down to the tunnel and kicking her way through. She came up in the front half of a lake. Five minutes later, she found the trampled area by the embankment where two people had struggled to put on clothes before finally stepping away.

It was full afternoon now. The sun hammered against her face until she could see each vein pumping blood across the thin layer of her eyelids. She replaced her flashlights on her utility belt. She checked the quantity and types of darts she had left.

She walked until she found a soft field of fresh grass and waving dandelions cradled by a silent forest. She curled up in a warm beam of sunlight, and like a panther, she slept.

In her dreams she saw her father, she saw her uncle. She pictured arsenic-laden birthday cakes. She remembered the first thrust of the insulin-loaded needle and the look of genuine surprise that had crossed the old man's face. Her dreams grew bigger, filling with violent reds and furious purples. She dreamed of the plague. She dreamed of people clutching their throats and screaming and dying from unknown agents they couldn't see, smell or taste.

She woke up. The dreams were safely tucked away again in the back of her mind where they weren't allowed to come out to play. She adjusted her utility belt, focused on the matter at hand and prepared for round two. She had a new plan.

Thirteen

"Okay, I'll go first." Jack jostled Josie aside with his shoulder, his hand closing over the front doorknob. His face was grim, his body poised for action.

"Do you really think she's here?"

"No, but we can't be too careful." He turned the knob, but it refused to budge. The door was still locked. They both grimaced.

"Great," Josie muttered. "I'm locked out of my own home. Hey, my feather bed is in there." For a moment, it appeared she was going to bang her fists against her front door in desperation. Jack grasped her hands quickly and dragged her around the side of the house before the neighbors began to peek out their windows at this early dawn display.

They'd gotten up at 4:00 a.m., restored by sleep and instantly tense. After a brief conference in the kitchen, Stone and Jack had agreed Stone would take Jessica up to his mountain retreat and Jack would try to set a trap for the hit woman at Jack's house. Stone would double back when he thought Jessica was safe and keep tabs on Josie. Jessica and Josie had agreed that Jessica would keep Stone occupied and Josie would assist Jack. It was her life, too. Now they were in search of fresh clothes and supplies at Josie's place.

"Spare key?" he whispered, trying to keep a low profile. Not many people were up and moving at 5:30 a.m. in Josie's neighborhood, and he wanted to keep it that way.

Just because he believed the assassin would be more likely to be watching his house—he, after all, had guns and essential supplies at his place—didn't mean he wanted to advertise their movements.

"Beneath the planter on the back porch."

"That's original."

"How was I supposed to know Grand Springs was suddenly going to be hosting a hit women convention? I thought of it as a quiet, friendly place."

They crept around back, retrieved her key from beneath the planter and attempted once more to enter her home.

"Okay, stand back."

"Tough guy," Josie grumbled, but she did move behind his back. In spite of her spirited words, he could feel the nervousness radiating from her. She stood closer than necessary, her hands brushing his back. Her blue eyes were wary in her pale face.

Jack took a deep breath. He had only Stone's spare gun, a Chief's Special, and he wished for a nine-millimeter. Or maybe a sawed-off shotgun. God, he didn't like doing this with Josie at his side. He wished he could've gotten her to stay put at Stone's place.

He turned the key, heard the lock click. He slipped the key into his pocket and gripped the knob securely. "Stay at my back," he whispered softly. "No sudden movements or unexpected noises. I'd hate to shoot you."

"I would hate that, too." Her voice had risen to an unnatural octave. Her fingers curled around the belt loops of his jeans.

He held the Chief's Special in front of him, safety off, and opened the door.

The entryway was dark and shadowed, the living room opening up on his right. The blinds were slanted shut and the just-rising sun too weak to do anything about it. He waited fifteen seconds for his eyes to adjust to the darkness. Then he scoured the room for any shapes or shadows that didn't belong.

The entryway was clear, the living room, as well. In front of them, the hallway leading to the back bedrooms yawned darkly.

Josie snapped on a light, and he was so jumpy he almost leapt out of his skin.

"No sudden movements, remember!"

"I couldn't see," she hissed back. "And...and it was *dark*."

He took a deep breath, trying to steady both of them. He couldn't remember ever feeling so edgy, but maybe that's because he was accustomed to lurking in dangerous places with Stone, who could fire a gun with the best of them. Now he had Josie, strong, stubborn Josie who deserved a helluva lot better than to be led skulking through her own home.

He placed his open palm against her belly and flattened her against the hallway wall. "Like this," he instructed softly. "Follow me."

He inched along the hallway, his gun held upright against his chest, his back against the wall, his shoulder brushing Josie's. There was no sound in the house, no movement. He heard only his own heartbeat and Josie's ragged breathing.

If the hit woman realized they had escaped, where would she try next? Here at Josie's house, trying to get the most important person first, or at his place, which was the more logical home for them to go? Or maybe she was already after Stone and Jessica, realizing that getting to them would bring Jack to her.

The sweat beaded up on his brow and trickled painstakingly slow down his cheek. And the end of the hallway, the ceiling light hit its limits and the shadows grew deep. Closer, closer, closer.

Was that breathing he heard in the silence? Was that annoying tick-tock some distant wall clock, or the sound of someone else's nervous heart beating too fast? Damn, damn, damn, he wanted Josie out of the way.

They drew up to the bedroom doorway. Jack no longer spoke. He straightened his arms, leading with his gun, and stepped into the doorway with a quick one hundred and eighty degree sweep. Left, center, right. Nothing moved, nothing stirred. The feather bed with its riotous bedspread sat alone and untouched. He stepped in quickly, checking behind the door, sweeping the bathroom. He drew back the shower curtain and in a moment of sheer lunacy, checked under the sink. The master bath was clear.

"Stay here," he told Josie firmly. She stood in the middle of her bedroom, her long blond hair spilling around her shoulders, her delicate features unnaturally pale. In Jessica's well-broken-in jeans and a long pink sweater, she looked too fragile and feminine for this kind of work. But her shoulders were set and her gaze was steady. His gaze went to her hands instinctively, for his mother's nervous ring-twisting was always the first sign of a "spell" coming on. Josie's hands were quiet, knit in front of her and held securely in place. His mother would be quivering with the strain by now. Marjorie probably would be yelling at him for putting her in such a position. Josie simply sized up the situation and helped him one hundred percent.

If something happened to her, he would be forced to violence, he was sure of it.

She let him go with a silent nod, her blue eyes strong and determined in the shadows. He stepped back into the silent hall, approaching the second bedroom with even more caution. They'd split up, the perfect time for an ambush. One quick dart and he would be out and Josie would be left unprotected.

He stepped grimly into the shadowed room, gun held

out and finger already tight on the trigger. *Come on, dammit. Show yourself and let's get this over with. Come out and face me!*

Nothing moved, nothing stirred. Josie's house was empty.

He didn't waste time on relief.

He stomped back to Josie's bedroom. "All right," he said briskly. "Grab a few supplies—whatever you feel you need. Then let's get you into a hotel."

Josie looked him straight in the eye. "No," she said firmly. "I have a better idea."

"What do you think? Does it simply scream 'I'm on the run' or what?" Josie held up a long black raincoat for inspection. She was humming merrily, quite pleased with herself. Jack was gnashing his teeth in her entryway.

"You are not doing this."

"And sunglasses, of course. Oooh, and a hat. A big, floppy hat. I know I have one here somewhere."

"You are going to a hotel where you will sit and wait."

"And a scarf. How about a red scarf? That ought to catch ol' Super Chick's eye. I'd hate to get all dressed up and not have her notice."

"Dammit, Josie—"

She shoved the raincoat, sunglasses and hat into his arms, already bustling down the hall in search of a scarf. She expected him to kick and scream for a bit. Jack Stryker seemed convinced that the rest of the world would never survive without him. But her idea was good, dammit, and she had no intention of sitting in some crummy hotel room, slowly losing her mind as she imagined Catwoman creeping up behind Jack and sticking some poisoned needle in his neck. No, they were in this together and she planned on doing her part. Jack said he wanted to set a trap. Well, no one knew more about traps than a con man's daughter.

She retrieved the scarf and walked back to him. His gaze had gone almost black with simmering rage and frustration. She simply ignored his mood. He'd get over it. "All right, here's the drill. We're betting she's watching your place because your place makes the most sense for us to seek out, right? I mean, two people on the run from a rabid hit woman need guns and supplies, not exactly the kinds of things an accountant keeps under her bed. So we scope out your place, waiting until dusk. I make a big production of 'sneaking into' your house while you keep watch. Evil Hit Woman, who's conscientiously keeping watch, will notice and follow. You grab her."

"What if she isn't keeping watch?" Jack ground out, his hands fisted at his side. "What if she's already in my house?"

"Hmm, good point. Okay, we'll have to scope out your house first and see if it's clear. I know, pretend you're a neighbor calling to report a burglary of Jack Stryker's house. The police will come and check out your house for you, without you ever having to reveal your identity or location." She beamed proudly, pleased with her idea.

For a moment, even Jack looked impressed. Immediately, he wiped the expression from his face and returned to scowling. "Okay. I'll do that. Now, you go to a hotel and sit tight."

"Now, Jack, that's no way to treat a modern woman. Particularly after everything we've been through."

"Josie, I don't want you in danger."

"I know, Jack." She looked at him steadily. "But that ship has sailed. I am in danger. We've got an assassin after us. Now, let's stop arguing and work together to do something about it."

"I will. You go to a hotel."

"Jack Stryker." She actually stomped her foot. "What kind of shallow, simpering female do you mistake me for?

Do you think I could stand sitting in a hotel worrying about you any more than you could sit in a hotel worrying about me? Dammit, I'm your partner. Part of loving me means accepting that. Let's face it. I don't exactly sit quietly very well. It's just not a strong suit of mine!''

"Well, I don't exactly toss the people I love in danger very well. It's just not a strong suit of mine!" he roared right back.

"Trust me to be tough!" she yelled.

"Trust me to take care of you!" he demanded.

"Dammit!" she cried, and stomped her foot again in frustration.

"Dammit," he agreed darkly. "And now I'm going to kiss you!"

"I know!"

He kissed her hard and then she kissed him back just as fiercely. The air heated up ten degrees and almost singed off their hair. They were both crazy. His hands shoved her head back, his mouth ate her lips. She suckled on his lower lip greedily and wrapped her arms around his shoulders. Just as harshly, he drew back.

"We'll do it my way," she stated without preamble, still breathing hard. She could hear her heart thundering in her chest. She felt slightly giddy, almost punch-drunk with adrenaline and fear and passion. In the shadows, she could see the intensity in his own gaze. Jack Stryker wasn't such a cool, calm Boy Scout anymore. He looked torn between strangling her with his bare hands and making love to her on her entryway floor.

"Face it," she said at last, "life with me will never be boring." Her chest was still heaving.

He grumbled something that sounded suspiciously like "damn, stubborn, idiot female" before he finally nodded his head curtly. No one ever said Stryker gave in gracefully. Abruptly, she grabbed his cheeks, lowering his head fiercely. She felt him tense, preparing for another onslaught, but she didn't attack him. She kissed him lingeringly, slowly and with a great deal of meaning. And his body relaxed and his arms curled around her waist and he tucked her against him.

Long after the kiss ended, he remained standing next to her, cradling her body, resting his cheek against her golden hair. "Be careful, Josie," he whispered at last. "Promise me you'll be careful."

"I'll be careful," she swore softly. "But it will be okay, Jack. After all, you'll be there, watching my back. You'll protect me. We'll be all right."

"Let's move," he said at last.

"Let's move."

From down the block, they watched two squad cars pull up to Jack's house after he used a pay phone to report a probable break-in. The sun was up, the sky clear, as the officers got out of their squad cars and perused Jack's half of the duplex he rented. They knocked on the door of the other apartment, but that owner was gone.

The officers circled the small house one more time. Jack watched them inspect the windows, then try the door. Everything seemed secure.

Eventually, the officers left.

Jack and Josie hunkered down for the afternoon in the back of Jessica's car, taking turns staring at the house and rolling down the windows to combat the heat. Finally, dusk arrived. The street filled momentarily with cars as people returned home from their workdays. Small, four-door vehicles and family station wagons pulled into modest-size homes and disgorged their bundles of children, dogs and sporting equipment.

Sounds of laughter and family conversation drifted down the street. From the third house on the right came the sound of a couple fighting over the newly arrived on-line bill. Then the sun sank all the way down, the couple made up, and families sat down to dinner.

The street became silent and shadowed once more, sturdy walls insulating the families of the neighborhood until they all lived together and yet remained alone.

It was time. Josie got up gingerly from the back seat of Jessica's car. She stretched out her legs, looked at Jack wordlessly one more time, then popped open the car door. She stepped out, squashing the floppy hat down onto her head.

Still nothing moved.

"Be careful!" Jack warned behind her one more time. She nodded, squared her shoulders and set out. She had Jack's key in her pocket.

From the car, Jack watched her round her shoulders and duck her head, imitating a thief skulking back to her lair. He held the Chief's Special on his lap, the safety off, his finger on the trigger. Sweat beaded down his cheek maddeningly slow, but he didn't wipe it away.

His attention was focused one hundred percent on Josie's approach of his house.

"Come on," he muttered. "Come on. Show yourself."

He raised his gun until the muzzle just rested on the top of the open window.

"Come on, dammit. I'm ready."

Josie looked from side to side. Her fingers dug into the deep pockets of the raincoat. She hunched over the door, a shadowy figure in black. After a moment, he saw the door crack open. She slipped through the opening as if she had no substance.

He waited. The assassin would show herself now. He would be ready.

The door closed behind Josie and she disappeared from sight.

* * *

Inside the house, Josie stopped long enough to take a deep breath. Jack's home smelled musty, and after a moment, her eyes adjusted enough to make out dark carpeting and dark furniture. It was not a cheery or comforting apartment. It was a space a cop rented so he would have a place to hang his gun at the end of a long day.

She kept her back to the wall, her ears alert for sounds of disturbance. The street seemed unnaturally silent. Her nerves stretched a little tighter.

"Come on," she whispered. "Come on, Super Chick. We're ready."

Nothing moved outside. Nothing moved inside.

After a moment, Josie moved deeper into the stale room. She wove in and out of the furniture. She wondered if she should go through the motions of gathering supplies, then make a big production of sneaking back out. Maybe that would make the assassin show.

Straight Arrow Stryker, however, probably kept his guns locked in a gun cabinet with the ammunition locked in a separate container. He hadn't given her keys for either, and she didn't have the talent to pick serious locks. She wandered into the kitchen.

And then she saw the note, hanging from the refrigerator in big, block letters.

DETECTIVE STRYKER:
LET'S MAKE A DEAL. I HAVE YOUR PARENTS. YOUR MOTHER SENDS HER REGARDS. COME TO THEIR PLACE. BRING YOUR FRIEND. IF YOU FOLLOW THE RULES AND DON'T CALL THE COPS, PERHAPS I'LL LET YOUR PARENTS LIVE.

There was no signature, the note didn't require one. Josie read it once, then twice, and then a third time before she could draw a breath. Dear God. Ben. Betty Stryker. Jack would go ballistic when he saw this.

And he would do exactly what the hit woman ordered, even though it would surely cost him his life. For his parents, he would do that. For Jack, love and honor and duty were too intertwined to ever be separated. He was everything her father hadn't been and the results could be just as tragic.

Josie had had too much of tragedy.

It only took her a minute to make up her mind. She knew where Ben lived. She found a back window of the duplex, knowing Jack was watching the front, and crawled out into the night.

"Think Josie, think. What would your father do?"

Jack hunkered down lower in the car, his eyes still peeled on the front door of the duplex. Slowly his gaze moved up the street, then back down. Nothing. Nothing. Nothing.

Seconds turned to minutes. A quarter of an hour passed. Was the assassin waiting for him to show himself and then she would move? What if the woman was somehow already in his house and now had Josie?

He made it five more minutes, then he couldn't take the strain. He had to know what was going on inside his house. He had to make sure Josie was all right.

He stepped outside of the car, gun ready, and approached the duplex.

Betty Stryker whimpered low in her throat, her large, dilated eyes focused on the black-clad woman pacing in their living room. The woman slanted her a sharp, annoyed look.

"Shhh," Ben said instantly, trying to soothe his wife the best he could with his hands tied around the back of

a chair. "It will be all right, honey. Jack will come, it will be all right."

Betty looked at him. He could see the sheen of sweat on her face and the panic rimming her eyes. Her heart was beating too fast and he saw the pulse at the base of her throat flutter like a butterfly.

Ben kept himself steady. "Deep breaths," he ordered calmly. "Deep breaths."

After a moment, Betty nodded. He saw her relax a fraction and he smiled his encouragement. Even after all these years, he felt his love for her knot his chest.

"We're gonna be all right," he promised solemnly. "We're gonna be all right."

In front of them, the strange woman with her beautiful features and cold, cold eyes kept pacing.

Josie had a helluva time flagging down a cab. Then she worried she would run out of money before arriving at Ben and Betty Stryker's street. They lived in a secluded, wooded area where house lots were measured in acres and things like streetlights and sidewalks were frowned upon. Finally, she thrust a wad of bills into the taxi driver's hand, fell out of the back seat and realized she'd arrived with no clear plan. She didn't have a gun, she didn't have training in negotiating for the release of hostages from psychopathic assassins. She didn't dare call the cops or the situation could deteriorate even worse.

Oh, God, she was the cavalry and she didn't even know how to ride a horse.

Distraction, she thought at last. She needed to create a diversion, something to get the hit woman out of Ben and Betty's house. When she was little, her father had taught her how to play any role from that of a little boy to a sick little girl. She knew how to be a salesman or a preacher or a pool shark. And she couldn't quite think how any of that would help her now, particularly as the hit woman would recognize her instantly if she approached the house.

She needed something better.

Josie's gaze fell on a woodpile behind the Strykers' house. Then she glanced at the big metal trash barrels. Finally, her gaze swept to the rooftop of the nearest neighboring house.

She set off at a dead run and arrived at the neighboring doorstep with a gasp.

"Fire!" She cried at the top of her lungs, pounding on the door. "Fire at the Strykers' place!"

"Oh, my God," the man gasped. He was already picking up the phone and dialing 911.

Josie leapt off his porch and was already running again. Okay. The fire department was on its way. Now, she just needed a fire.

In the murky darkness of the kitchen, Jack read the note. He did not swear, he did not yell, he did not pray. He turned, his expression set in stone, and he walked out of the house to Jessica's car.

Five seconds later, he was peeling down the street and flooring it to his parents' house.

"Josie, you fool!"

"I...I smell smoke." Betty's voice cracked the silence unnaturally high, making all of them flinch. "I do. I really do."

Ben was already groaning, trying desperately to reach out but unable to. He fought the ropes in a moment of panic, seeing the woman turn around with a look of pure, cold menace on her face. She raised her strange-looking gun and leveled it at his wife.

"Wait!" Ben cried hoarsely. His thick fingers tangled with the ropes. Then abruptly, he stilled. He frowned and sniffed the air. His eyes widened. "I'll be damned. It's smoke, all right. We're on fire!"

Josie took off her raincoat and used it to fan the flames in the metal trash bin higher and higher. She threw in some wet leaves and the smoke turned dark and oily. She billowed it some more until her eyes stung and her lungs burned.

She lit the second trash barrel using the lighter she'd found next to the grill, then the third. The night sky was becoming hazy, the crackling grew loud. The heat was fierce enough to bloom sweat all over her body and the flames bright enough to light up the back of the house like a football field.

"Come on, nice and thick. We need a bit of a show here."

She peeled her ears for the sound of fire department sirens and kept the trash fires building. At the first sign of approach, she was gonna tip these babies over. The fire department would storm the scene, and if the hit woman had an ounce of survival instinct, she would flee immediately.

At least, Josie hoped so.

Abruptly, the back screen door of the house slid open.

Jack gunned Jessica's poor car down the street. Before him, he saw dark plumes suddenly thread up above the night-shrouded trees, flickering red flames lighting their way.

Oh, my God, there was a fire.

He slammed the gas pedal all the way to the floor and bullied the car around the corner.

From behind him, he heard the sound of sirens splitting the air.

* * *

The woman appeared, inch by inch, the barrel of her tranquilizer gun leading the display. For a horrible moment, Josie froze, not sure what to do. She hadn't planned on this yet. She wasn't ready yet!

Sirens cut through the smoky sky. She saw the woman freeze, then slowly stepped back toward the house.

No! The woman couldn't go back into the house. She was supposed to get out of the house. She was supposed to abandon her hostages. Dammit!

Josie did the only thing she could think of. She bounded out from behind the tree and sprinted across the backyard, the light of the flames putting her in plain view.

"Jack, start the engine!" she yelled. "Jack, start the engine!"

And she knew the precise moment she had the woman's attention because the first poisoned dart whistled by her ear.

Jack slammed the brake to the floor, stopping so fast the car fishtailed drunkenly before he brought it under control. Half a block from his parents' wooded home, the smoke was thick enough to sting his eyes, and he could feel the heat radiating out in waves. The sirens blared louder and louder, the fire department descending upon the area.

What if their arrival caused the assassin to panic and kill his parents? Or Josie? God, what had she done this time?

His gun in his hand, he abandoned the car and ran toward the heat.

"Damn!" Josie ducked, but the dart passed by close enough for her to imagine its sting. She raced away from the flames, desperate for the cover of night once more. She had the woman out of the house. She had the fire department arriving. Surely they would knock on the door, discover Mr. and Mrs. Stryker and get them out of there. They'd tell them about the woman, the police would be called, and help would arrive.

Josie just had to keep the woman entertained for say, ten, fifteen, twenty minutes. She'd managed to elude Catwoman all day and all night before. What was twenty minutes?

The next dart buried itself in the brush above her ear, and Josie bolted forward two steps faster. God, her side hurt. She plunged deeper into the forest, tripped over a tree branch and went sprawling. Gasping for breath, she heaved herself up and stumbled forward.

She couldn't see a damn thing anymore. The night was too thick. The smoke hurt her eyes. Why wasn't it slowing the woman down? She was shooting with uncanny accuracy given the conditions.

What about night vision goggles?

That sounded like something Super Chick would have brought along for this mission. After all, she'd had time to recover and retrieve supplies just as they had. Josie began to giggle hysterically as still she ran.

Jack thundered up the stairs of the back porch. Now he could see that three trash bins were burning, close enough together to give off intense heat. Josie must have lit them, but to what purpose?

He flattened himself against the back wall of his parents' house, straining his ears for sound above the cackle and pop of burning wood.

His mother was sobbing. His father was soothing her with low murmurs. His palms began to sweat. Damn, where was Josie? Worse, where was the assassin?

He heard a sound from the forest behind his parents' house. A low thud of someone falling. The crunch of leaves as someone else ran.

"Help!" his father cried out. "Help, we're in here."

"Dad?" Jack called out. "Are you alone?"

"The woman's out there," Ben yelled immediately, understanding what his son needed to know. "Watch your back!"

Jack heard the sound of more leaves crunching, then the sound of twigs snapping. Then the sirens grew too loud for him to hear anything. The fire department had arrived.

He sprang off the front porch and raced toward the first vehicle.

"Detective Stryker, Grand Springs police!" he screamed at the first startled firefighter. "Three trash cans burning around back. Two civilians tied up in the house. Get your EMTs in there immediately. The woman has a nervous condition. Give me that."

He grabbed a heavy-duty flashlight from the stock in the fire truck, and while the head firefighter yelled "Wait!" Jack once more began to run.

Josie halted behind a tree. Her breath was so labored, it hurt to inhale. She hunched closer to the tree trunk. She couldn't see anything, and the fire department's sirens were too loud for her to hear anything.

Then abruptly, as if reading her thoughts, the fire department cut the sirens. In the suddenly descending silence, all the other sounds rushed in on her.

Breathing. Heavy breathing. Right on the other side of the tree trunk.

She froze. She swallowed her next breath and squeezed her eyes shut as sweat popped out of her pores.

The assassin had found her. One more step around the tree trunk and the woman would turn, see her and fire the gun. At this close range, she couldn't miss.

Tree branch, tree branch. Grab a weapon, Josie. Grab a rock!

But as she bent down, the woman moved. Suddenly she was right in front of Josie, a preternatural figure swathed all in black with a pair of goggles distorting her eyes. Only her hair, pale and silvery, glowed in the moonlight.

"No," Josie whimpered, too scared to move.

The woman raised her gun. For one brief moment, the corners of her mouth lifted and Joanna Jackson smiled.

"Finally," she murmured, and leveled the tranquilizer gun.

Jack, I'm so sorry. I'm so, so sorry.

The woman squeezed the trigger and gunfire peeled through the hot, smoky air.

Fourteen

"How do you feel?"

The voice penetrated gentle and soft but it still made her temples throb. Josie groaned, trying to burrow back down into the blessed cocoon of unconsciousness.

"Her color's returning." This voice was slightly more anxious. Jack's voice. In spite of steady beats of pain drumming against her forehead, she smiled.

"Here she comes," the first voice said. "Josie. Josie Reynolds. Blink if you can hear me."

She blinked, but it was only grudgingly. In the velvet softness of semiconsciousness, she was finally getting the rest she was sure she deserved.

"Josie? Josie, how do you feel?"

Reluctantly, she peeled open her eyes. The air was still smoky, and she flared her nostrils when she inhaled. Above her, red-and-blue lights whirled around and around and around. The fire engines. And police cars. Apparently, she was lying flat on the ground. Jack was leaning over her, his face heavily lined with concern. An EMT was also at her side, now taking her pulse. She saw Ben sitting with Mrs. Stryker in the background, cradling his wife against his chest and rubbing her arms.

"How is she?" Josie asked automatically.

The EMT frowned, but Jack understood immediately. His face relaxed at the sound of her rough, rasping voice and he hunkered down closer.

"Better," he said quietly. "She was a bit shaken up,

but she refused to take the drugs the doctor offered and she seems to be calming down on her own. She and my father are a lot tougher sometimes than I give them credit for." His gaze grew soft. "How are you, Josie?"

She blinked a few more times, tested out all her limbs and discovered she was alive, after all. "Not bad for a woman who's been running up mountainsides, spelunking caves, traversing underground lakes, and then playing cat and mouse with an assassin. What did she hit me with?"

"Nothing."

"Nothing?"

"You fainted."

"What?" She mustered all her dignity. "I most certainly did not! A Reynolds never faints!"

"Fear of imminent death sometimes has that effect on people. It's perfectly understandable."

She scowled. "Well, if I fainted, why aren't I dead?" she asked bluntly.

"I shot her."

"You shot her?"

"In the shoulder. We have her in police custody now. The doctor has assured us that the wound isn't serious. Probably we can begin questioning her as early as tomorrow."

"Oh, well, this is just great! In the face of danger, I faint, you shoot a gun. I'm a miserable excuse as a sidekick."

"You're a perfect sidekick," he said honestly. "While trying to burn down the neighborhood was slightly unorthodox, it did work. If you hadn't lured her out of the house like that, I'm not sure what would've happened."

She was mollified enough to try to sit up. The rescue worker and Jack immediately moved to assist.

"You're fine," the rescue worker said shortly. "No major injuries that I can tell. Get a good night's rest, take some aspirin if you have a headache and, well, stop chasing criminals. You'll be as good as new by the end of the week.''

"Mmm-hmm.'' Josie wasn't really paying attention to him anymore. Her gaze was locked on Jack. She finally gave up and curled her hand around his cheek, sighing at the lovely feel of his skin against hers. "You did it, Jack. You saved the world.''

"We did it,'' he corrected her mildly. "You really did help, Josie. Your point about teamwork and trust still stands. Of course, there is the small matter of you running off on your own after giving me such lectures on the subject—''

"I learned it from you!'' she interrupted hastily.

"Well, maybe we ought to learn from each other. Stick together, help each other out. Partnership?''

"Love?'' she whispered hopefully.

"Love,'' he promised gently.

He gathered her against his chest and held her dearly.

It took a week to sort everything out. Stone and Jessica returned from the mountains, Stone grumbling about missing all the fun. He got to spend the first session questioning Joanna Jackson, however, as Jack was still recovering. Most of the recovery involved lying in Josie's feather bed, sleeping soundly and working on his popcorn-catching technique. By Tuesday, he could catch three out of four kernels in his mouth, which was better than Josie, so she kicked him out and told him to get back to work.

After a few more rounds of passionate sex, he managed to do just that.

Jack, however, discovered he didn't have any better luck with Joanna Jackson than Stone did.

"Do you understand that we've run your prints? We have a match with warrants issued for various aliases in seven different states. You're in a lot of trouble. You're facing some pretty serious charges. Help us out here, and maybe we can do something for you.''

She merely regarded him coolly, as elegant and composed in an orange prison suit as a person could be. Not even the sling decorating her arm detracted from her confidence.

''You killed Olivia Stuart. You framed Josie Reynolds. Then you set out to kill both Josie and me. Who hired you, Joanna?''

''Santa Claus.''

''Come on, you're a young, attractive female. According to our findings, you drive the right car and reside in the finest hotels. I don't really think you would enjoy prison much, Joanna.''

She shrugged, her blues eyes betraying nothing.

Jack leaned back, crossed his ankles up on the table and adopted her own negligent pose. ''So it's worth it to you? You'd go to jail rather than finger who hired you?''

''A girl's gotta have her professionalism, or she has nothing at all.''

''Do you love him, Joanna, is that it? Was this case personal, a favor for a 'friend.' ''

''I don't have friends.''

''Funny. I certainly wouldn't take the fall for an enemy.''

''I don't have enemies. At least not any who are still living.''

''Then, you'd go to jail for a stranger?''

She said nothing, but her expression was more appraising.

Jack dropped his feet to the ground in the interrogation room and leaned forward. ''Why did they want Olivia killed? Was it personal? Was it professional?''

''I didn't ask.''

"Come on. Were you approached by an individual, by a corporation? From what we've pieced together, you seem to work mostly for private individuals."

"I work for whoever can afford me."

"You're very expensive, aren't you, Joanna?"

"Quality costs."

"If I wanted to hire you, what would it take? Hundreds, thousands, tens of thousands?"

"One hundred thousand," she said coolly, "for an unguarded target. Up to seven digits, depending on the level of security and sophistication required."

"Olivia Stuart had no security. She was easy money, wasn't she?"

"Yes. As a matter of fact, she was."

Jack's eyes narrowed. He couldn't stop the bolt of anger. "The cleanup, though," he said tightly, "bet you lost a bundle on that."

Her eyes narrowed. "Yes," she said curtly. "But sometimes it's like that."

"Check is in the mail, is that how it works, Joanna?"

"Cash up front."

"Oh, of course. You probably don't trust anyone enough for checks. Too bad you can't spend the money. Too bad you'll be sitting in maximum security on a cement bed for the next twenty-five years. By the time you get out and access your Swiss bank accounts, you're not going to be so young or pretty anymore. You'll be too old to work as an assassin and not trained for anything else. You'll have no family, no friends. My guess is, by that point, you'll miss prison."

She turned away.

"Tough life, isn't it?" Jack hammered. "Never close to anyone. No family, no community, no boyfriends. All you have is your money and your lifestyle. Just the nice clothes and imported automobiles to keep you warm at night. And now you won't even have that. Just so you can protect some people you don't give a damn about. Your professionalism's worth that much, Joanna? You know none of your former clients are going to visit you in prison or send you cards on Christmas."

"I don't know who hired me," she said abruptly. Her gaze was fastened on the far wall.

"What do you mean? I hardly think you take orders from anonymous voices over the telephone."

She finally met his gaze. Her eyes were stormy, the only emotion he'd ever seen her express. "Dean Springer. He's the one who called, he's the one who showed up and briefed me. He gave me the files and the orders and he handed over the cash. He wanted me to take care of the Hanson woman, too, but I told him I wasn't risking everything for a silly vision...there are hundreds of tall blondes in Grand Springs. But for an extra fifty thousand, I did agree to framing Josie Reynolds. Planting the syringe, mailing packages to the cops.... It wasn't hard. At least not in the beginning."

"Who is Dean Springer?" Jack demanded.

She smiled benignly. "No one," she whispered. "Absolutely no one."

She hadn't lied to them. By the end of the week, they'd gotten an arrest warrant for Dean Springer, but he'd fled from his home. Dean had no degree, no expertise. He was a "neighborhood man." The kind of guy who grew up with people who went on to do interesting things. People who then hired him to do interesting things.

As Stone put it, he wasn't the general, but just another foot soldier. In short, they'd caught the person who'd pulled the trigger, but they still didn't know who had ordered Olivia's death or why.

The good news was that Josie's name was finally cleared. Hal Stuart publicly acknowledged that the audit had revealed Josie to be an excellent treasurer, and the mayor's office was happy to have her back.

Monday, she would return to work. Life would return to normal. Kind of.

Thursday night, Jack had dinner with his parents. Ben was his usual effervescent self. Betty was slightly anxious, but Jack saw her gaze going to his father time and time again. There was a new softness around her eyes, a new glow to her face. Their ordeal hadn't fractured his mother. It seemed to have given her more faith. Perhaps she'd realized what Ben had been saying all along. Life was messy, and families worked together to clean it up.

Jack thought his father was a very smart man. So Friday night, he decided he'd waited long enough. He put on his best suit, stopped by the jeweler's and visited the florist. He was ready.

Josie was still yawning when the doorbell rang. This recovery business was hard work, and everyone knew she took her job seriously. If she slept anymore, she was going to sink so deep into her feather mattress they would never find her body. She hadn't even bothered to get dressed for three consecutive days. She loved decadence.

Belting her red kimono robe more tightly around her waist, she wandered to her front door and spied one sharp-looking Jack Stryker through the peephole. Already she was smiling.

"Who is it?" she called out playfully.

"A moderate Republican in search of a good time."

"I think that's an oxymoron," she informed him, but opened the door gamely. Jack promptly withdrew the dozen peach roses from behind his back and held them out.

"I believe you requested these."

"Oh, oh my. Okay, you can come in and play."

She bustled away to put the roses in water. They were the real thing, complete with huge thorns and a wonderfully fresh scent. She didn't have any vases so she stuck the dozen in a canning jar after clipping off the ends. Her first bouquet of fresh roses.

"Nice day at the office, dear?" she teased, arranging her flowers.

Jack sighed and appeared momentarily disgruntled. "No progress," he grumbled. "Joanna will serve time for the murder, but we haven't moved beyond that. We still don't know why, Josie. Someone paid one hundred thousand dollars for Olivia's death and fifty to frame you. That's pretty darn serious money, and we don't know who and we don't know why. Hell, we don't even know if it was something personal or something professional."

Josie didn't answer. She didn't know, either. Olivia had been her best friend, but she had been a private person. Not even her children, Hal or Eve, seemed to know much about Olivia's personal life.

"Well," Jack said at last, his tone more brisk. "We'll catch up with this Dean Springer character sooner or later, and with a bit of pressure, I'm sure he'll give up his boss. We'll find him. Now, my dear—" he swept her close to him "—I didn't come here just to talk about work."

"No?" She ran her finger down his chest, toying with one of the pearly buttons. "What did you come here for?" she asked as innocently as possible. A rich warmth was already coursing through her.

"Dinner."

"Dinner?"

"Yes, I believe I still have some making up to do. If memory serves, we discussed flowers—" he waved to the peach roses "—and fine dining. Hmm, you might want to change clothes."

He patted her silk robe, then realized she wasn't wearing

anything beneath it and became a little distracted. With effort, he drew back. "Why don't you put on a dress, Josie. I have dinner reservations at the finest restaurant imaginable."

"Randolphs?"

"Better."

Puzzled and amused, Josie retreated to her room long enough to get dressed. Stryker in a romantic mood was pretty hard to resist. She settled on the black skirt and white silk blouse she'd wanted to wear on their first date a few weeks ago. She was rewarded by the frank appreciation darkening Stryker's eyes. Not bad at all.

He didn't drive her to Randolphs. He drove them out of town, then kept heading up the mountain. Abruptly, he pulled over. Josie looked around in bewilderment.

"Uh, Jack. There's nothing here."

"That's what you think."

He opened the car door for her, took her hand and led her straight into the woods. They had to walk slowly, her black suede heels not exactly cut out for this business. Abruptly, the trees broke, revealing a gentle lake rippling with moonlight and deep mountain grass swaying with the breeze. The sky stretched out like rich velvet above them, sprinkled lavishly with stars and winking like a child. In the distance, an owl pulsed the air with "whoo, whoo. Whoo, whoo."

A picnic table was set up by the shore. Jack flared a match, and a minute later, two candles flickered brightly from their sterling silver bases.

"Oh, my." Josie sighed.

Jack had obviously given this some thought. The picnic table was covered in fine linen and heavy with silver serving platters and thin china plates. The benches on both sides had been covered with cushions.

"Your chair," Jack said grandly, obviously quite pleased with himself.

Josie sat, inspecting the dishes and discovering an exquisite fare of chilled shrimp cocktails, spinach salad and poached dill salmon. The last platter contained a lush array of sweet ripe strawberries dipped in chocolate.

"Will you father my children?" Josie murmured, completely awestruck. "Seriously."

"I'll think about it." Now Jack was definitely smug.

He served her first, then himself, and they both ate with lusty appreciation of fine food. There was chilled white wine and thick crystal glasses filled with water. Of course, some small buggy things committed hari-kari in the candles, but it really was a perfect dinner.

"I thought you would like outdoors," Jack said at last, finishing off his salmon, wiping his mouth with the linen napkin and pushing back his plate. "Given all our quality time in caves."

"I certainly have a new appreciation for open spaces," Josie assured him. She took his hand. "Jack, this was perfect."

"I wanted to do something special, Josie. I wanted to show you just how much you mean to me."

She opened her mouth, but he silenced her by placing a finger over her lips. "There's one last thing, you know."

She raised a brow in silent question.

"I gave you flowers, I presented you with a fine dinner. But I believe you also mentioned precious gems. Yes, exactly. You said after flowers and dinner, my apology would have to move on to precious gems. Well, I'd hate to disappoint."

He reached into his jacket pocket. His fingers were trembling slightly and his stomach had tied into knots. He didn't doubt what he was doing for a moment, however.

He drew out the blue velvet ring box, and very carefully, he opened it.

The solitaire diamond winked in the moonlight and burned with an inner flame.

"Josie Reynolds, will you marry me?"

Josie stared at the diamond. She stared at Jack. She struggled very hard to say *"Yes!"* but only succeeded in working her mouth like a blowfish.

"Take a drink of wine," Jack suggested.

She drained her glass. "Yes!" she burst out. "Definitely yes. Of course, yes. Oh, oh, this is so perfect!"

She scrambled out of the picnic bench, running her nylons but too excited to care. Jack caught her against him before she toppled them both to the ground and returned her kisses just as passionately.

"I love you, Josie."

"I love you, Stryker."

He slipped the ring on her finger while the moon rippled across the lake and the owls murmured their consent.

*   *   *   *   *

Alicia Scott is a regular contributor to our
Silhouette Sensation® series. Look out for
her next novel!

36 Hours

When disaster turns to passion

continues with

NINE MONTHS

by Beverly Barton
available in August

Here's an exciting preview…

Nine Months

The elevator doors swung open. Paige Summers took a step forward, then halted. Since it was after office hours, she had expected the elevator to be empty. It wasn't. One lone man occupied the small space, tall and lean, with an aura of masculine strength surrounding him. Easing his big body forward, he stood up straight. "If you're worried about getting on an elevator alone with a stranger, I can assure you that you'll be safe with me."

The man wasn't local. He spoke with a drawl. Oklahoma or Texas, maybe, she thought. Definitely not the Deep South. Paige forced a smile to her lips. "I'm sorry. It's just that I didn't expect anyone to still be here." She stepped inside the elevator and the elevator doors closed.

Jared Montgomery couldn't remember the last time he'd been instantly attracted to a woman, and never such a strong attraction. She was lovely, in a young, fresh, unspoiled sort of way, and every inch of her five-and-a-half-foot body was filled out in lush, curvaceous proportions. He figured she was somebody's secretary. As a general rule, he didn't date out of his social circle, but for this gorgeous woman, he'd make an exception.

The elevator jolted to a sudden halt, tossing Jared sideways, directly against the young woman. Acting purely on instinct, he grabbed her the moment he realized they were both falling. She clutched the front of his shirt, ripping off two buttons. Jared maneuvered her quickly, taking the brunt of the fall himself.

The red emergency lights came on instantly. Paige realized she was lying on top of the stranger, her body intimately aligned with his. Her breasts crushed against his muscular chest. Their bellies pressed together. Their legs entwined....

Grand Springs was a flurry of activity on Monday morning when Jared arrived at the new office of his Colorado branch of Montgomery Real Estate and Land Development. He had decided to cut his visit short. The thirty-six hour blackout upon his arrival had set the tone for the entire weekend. One wild, unexpected event after another. He'd said his goodbyes to Paige, telling himself that he'd forget all about her. But he'd dreamed about her. About touching her. Kissing her. Making love to her. For the past two days, he hadn't been able to get her out of his mind.

Since Grand Springs wasn't that big a town, the longer he stayed, the greater the odds were that he and Paige would run into each other. He didn't want that, and he suspected neither did she. What had happened between them had been a chance happening, a one-night stand to end all one-night stands.

"I didn't expect you until later in the day." Greg Addison sauntered into Jared's private office.

"Since I'm only going to be here a couple of days," Jared said, "I need to meet and break in my new secretary. You did hire someone for me, didn't you?"

"Yes. As a matter of fact, Ms. Summers has just arrived. She's outside talking to my assistant, Kay Thompson."

"Well, I might as well meet them now. I want to brief my secretary on her duties before I go."

Moments later the two men emerged from L. J. Montgomery's office.

"This is Ms. Thompson, my assistant, and Ms. Summers, your secretary," Greg said.

"Ms. Thompson." Smiling at the tall, slender brunette, Jared held out his hand, then turned to her companion.

"And this must be—" Jared stared at the curvaceous redhead who was looking at him as if he had suddenly sprung a second head. Dear God, it couldn't be. But it was. Ms. Summers was Paige. His Paige…from the elevator…

October 6

After hurriedly leaving Grand Springs four months ago, L. J. Montgomery was finally returning. Paige couldn't help but wonder if Jared had stayed away because of her. Surely not. He'd made it clear that their encounter in the elevator had been a mistake, something to be forgotten. Easy enough for him. But not for her.

Paige realized that once she discovered L. J. Montgomery and her lover, Jared, were one in the same she should have given up her job as his secretary. If only she'd done the smart thing, she wouldn't have had to endure talking to him on the phone, which always prompted her to dream about him. And she wouldn't be facing the prospect of his imminent return.

But now that she was in this situation, she desperately needed her good medical insurance to pay the doctor and hospital bills. This situation? She laughed aloud and tears sprung to her eyes. She'd been able to keep her condition a secret from everyone at work, including Kay Thompson. She wasn't showing—not yet—not so that anyone could tell she was four months pregnant. But sooner or later, her pregnancy would become noticeable, and then what would she tell everyone? What would she tell Jared?

Maybe she would feel differently about him once she saw him. It was possible that he wasn't as wonderful as she remembered. Maybe he was just an ordinary, attractive man with a nice smile. Paige heard Jared's voice in the hallway, then the door to her office swung open and he entered, followed by Greg Addison and Kay. Paige's heart stopped for a split second as she rose from her chair, her gaze riveted on him. When he paused briefly at her side, her smile widened. "Welcome back to Grand Springs," she said, amazed she'd been able to keep the nervous quiver out of her voice.

Looking at him, she wondered how on earth she was going to continue working for him, day after day, growing bigger and bigger with his child, and act as if he meant nothing more to her than an employer....

COMING NEXT MONTH

THE BADDEST BRIDE IN TEXAS
Maggie Shayne

Heartbreaker/The Brand Family

Two years ago, Kirsten Cowan had jilted Adam Brand and married the richest, meanest man in Texas—for reasons she was forced to keep secret. Now she stood accused of her husband's murder and she still couldn't tell the whole truth—even though Adam defied his own family to take her into hiding…

MURPHY'S LAW Marilyn Pappano

Evie DesJardiens had loved Jack Murphy with a reckless hunger. But when it had come to a choice between her and his career as a cop—he'd picked his job! Now he was back, asking for help with a murder investigation. She knew she shouldn't trust this man again—but she couldn't refuse him…*anything*!

EVERYDAY, AVERAGE JONES
Suzanne Brockmann

Tall, Dark and Dangerous

Navy SEAL Harlan Jones had rescued hostage Melody Evans in a daring and dangerous mission. Afterwards there had been a rush of excitement, relief and passion—a passion which left Melody with more than just memories! Now Jones was facing his toughest challenge yet: persuading Melody to marry him!

ONE MORE KNIGHT Kathleen Creighton

Years ago, Charlene Phelps had been talked into giving her baby up for adoption. But on a visit home she saw a photo of him. Was it possible someone knew where he was? In desperation she called an old friend—but it was Troy Starr who picked up the phone. And he refused to leave her side until she was reunited with her son.

COMING NEXT MONTH FROM

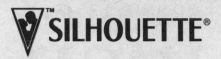 **SILHOUETTE**®

Intrigue
Danger, deception and desire

SOMEBODY'S BABY Amanda Stevens
SPENCER'S SECRET Laura Gordon
THE MISSING HOUR Dawn Stewardson
MYSTERY DAD Leona Karr

Special Edition
Compelling romances packed with emotion

OPERATION: BABY Barbara Bretton
THE WINNING HAND Nora Roberts
A FAMILY KIND OF GIRL Lisa Jackson
FROM HOUSE CALLS TO HUSBAND Christine Flynn
PRENUPTIAL AGREEMENT Doris Rangel
AKA: MARRIAGE Jule McBride

Desire
Provocative, sensual love stories

SLOW-TALKING TEXAN Mary Lynn Baxter
DEDICATED TO DEIRDRE Anne Marie Winston
THE CONSUMMATE COWBOY Sara Orwig
THE NON-COMMISSIONED BABY Maureen Child
COWBOYS DO IT BEST Eileen Wilks
THE TEXAS RANGER AND THE TEMPTING TWIN
Pamela Ingrahm

9907